RIDE THE MAN DOWN

OTHER FIVE STAR WESTERN TITLES BY BILL BROOKS:

The Messenger (2009)
Blood Storm (2012)
Frontier Justice (2012)
Winter Kill (2013)

A JOHN HENRY COLE STORY

RIDE THE MAN DOWN

BILL BROOKS

FIVE STAR
A part of Gale, Cengage Learning

GALE
CENGAGE Learning®

Detroit • New York • San Francisco • New Haven, Conn • Waterville, Maine • London

GALE
CENGAGE Learning·

LIBRARY OF CONGRESS CATALOGING-IN-PUBLICATION DATA

Brooks, Bill, 1943–
    Ride the man down : a John Henry Cole story / By Bill Brooks.
— First Edition.
        pages cm. -- (A John Henry Cole story)
        ISBN-13: 978-1-4328-2708-3 (hardcover)
        ISBN-10: 1-4328-2708-1 (hardcover)
        1. Private investigators—Fiction. I. Title.
PS3552.R65863R526 2013
813'.54—dc23   2013021211

First Edition. First Printing: November 2013.
Published in conjunction with Golden West Literary Agency.
Find us on Facebook– https://www.facebook.com/FiveStarCengage
Visit our website– http://www.gale.cengage.com/fivestar/
Contact Five Star™ Publishing at FiveStar@cengage.com

Printed in Mexico
1 2 3 4 5 6 7 17 16 15 14 13

Ride the Man Down

PROLOGUE

Indian Territory
1875

The Indian's woman was standing at the edge of the cornfield when she shot John Henry Cole. Moments before, he had placed the barrel of his Peacemaker just behind the Indian's ear. The press of cold steel seemed to do little to disturb his drunken sleep. He smelled like the bottom of a whiskey barrel. That, and wild onions. Strike a match, Cole figured, and they'd both go up in flames.

The Indian's name was Lucky Baker. But it wasn't the Indian Cole was after. That was a white man named Caddo Pierce. Pierce was wanted for illegally peddling his snakehead whiskey to the Indians and pimping a fourteen-year-old half-breed girl throughout the Nations. Cole had a fugitive warrant in his hip pocket issued from Judge Parker's court for Pierce's arrest. Cole already had four other prisoners chained in his wagon, a load of sorry souls he was taking back to Fort Smith to stand trial for various misdeeds. All of them white trash. Caddo Pierce was the last one on Cole's list and Cole didn't intend to go back across the Arkansas River without him.

"Wake up, Lucky," he ordered the Indian.

"*Mmmmm. . . .*" Lucky fluttered his lips, opened one eye, closed it again as though Cole was a troublesome insect he was enduring.

Cole shook him again and thumbed back the hammer on the

Peacemaker—a sound that usually got attention, even if the person was cold-cocked by whiskey. But Lucky hadn't come around. Cole swung a foot against the hammock the Indian was sleeping in and spilled him on the ground. He hit hard. That woke him up. He cursed and spat dirt and came up to his feet, swinging like a soft-brained prize fighter. Cole stuck the pistol in his face and said: "Don't be stupid." That had a sobering effect on the Indian and he stopped swinging, looking down the long barrel of the revolver until his eyes crossed. "Where's Caddo Pierce, that spit-for-brains brother-in-law of yours?" Cole asked.

Lucky's eyes uncrossed and rolled, then he saw the other men, the ones chained in the prison wagon, watching him. In spite of their own misfortune they were enjoying the show. Lucky stammered and toed the dirt and said he didn't know anything about the white man.

"Don't waste any more of my morning," Cole said. "You can either tell me where Pierce is, or you can climb in that wagon with those other jacklegs and come with me to Fort Smith in his place. Which will it be?"

"I don't know where Caddo's at, Deputy. Honest."

"The hell you don't."

A man can lie to you all day long with his mouth, but his eyes will give him away every time. Cole was looking into those eyes when he saw them shift to something over Cole's left shoulder. Cole knew he'd made a mistake. He was still turning, the pistol in his hand, when he saw her, standing there at the edge of the cornfield. She had what looked to be an old Springfield musket that was as long as she was tall and she had it aimed at Cole with the barrel dancing small circles in the air.

It all happened quickly, but slowly. In that spare bitter moment that took no longer than a breath, Cole's finger hesitated. Even his gunfighter's instinct wouldn't let him shoot a woman.

So, she shot Cole instead.

The ball hit Cole just below the collar bone and spun him sideways. Then the ground came up fast and he could taste dirt and something metallic, like a copper penny. Judging by the impact, it was one of those large bores, a .51 caliber, maybe. It stung. He looked at his outstretched hand and saw that he'd dropped his pistol somewhere in the tall weeds. He looked round, saw Lucky running, darting like a rabbit. Lucky joined up with the woman, and Cole watched helplessly as they ran into the cornfield, the stalks waving like a wind was passing through them, their dry leaves rustling against the heat.

The men chained in the wagon whooped and cheered like they'd just been given the keys to a whorehouse as Cole rolled over and saw his blood pool in the dust. Then for a time, he lay there, staring up at the sky, trying to suck in air and wondering if the bullet had nicked a lung. If it had, he was probably a dead man.

Cole noticed how deep blue and endless the world above him seemed to be. Time felt like it had stopped and he thought: *So this is what dying is all about.* Then he closed his eyes and saw red in the darkness.

He might have been out a minute, maybe an hour. "Is he dead?" he heard one of the prisoners ask. "Damn' sure looks like maybe he is," said another. "Well, that's mighty good news, then."

"How's it good news?"

"We ain't going to Fort Smith," the first one said. Ned Dicks, Cole thought it was, by the sound of his raspy voice. Somebody had tried to hang Dicks once but the rope broke in time to leave him with nothing more than a bum neck and a scratchy throat.

"That means ol' Parker ain't gonna be sendin' us up to the House of Corrections in Detroit."

"Why you damn' twit. If that deputy's dead, we're in a pickle. The damn' wolves will come and eat us, chained up here helpless as chickens! Either that or some other damn' deputy the judge has roaming 'round these parts will find us."

"Wolves?" someone else said. It sounded to Cole like the kid that had been running with Ned Dicks, with long yellow hair and gapped teeth.

Cole opened his eyes and sat up. The prisoners hooted. Cole was leaking blood like a busted spigot.

"Hell, he ain't dead!" The kid's voice sounded utterly disappointed.

"Well, that's good news, then."

"How's it good news?"

"The wolves won't come and eat us now."

"Jesus Christ! Ain't none of you boys got the brains God gave a goose?" It was Ned Dicks again. More hoots, some uneasy laughter.

Cole took stock of the wound. In spite of all the blood, it seemed like a clean shot through and through. A soft lead bullet like those old muskets fired, if it hits a bone, shatters and busts you up pretty good. Cole had seen many men in the war lose an arm or a leg because the surgeons couldn't repair shattered bones caused by Minié balls. He coughed, saw no blood in his spittle, and knew the bullet had missed his lungs.

Cole searched the weeds for his Peacemaker, found it, and jammed it into his belt. The men in the wagon watched him like caged monkeys watching a banana. Cole took the key from his pocket, unlocked the wrist irons of the callow youth that ran with Ned Dicks, and ordered him down. "There's an extra clean shirt in my kit there under the wagon seat. Take it out and tear it up into bandages."

"What in hell should I help you for?" the boy said, then looked up at the others for approval, to show them what a tough *hombre* he was.

"Don't make me say it twice," Cole warned. The kid seemed uncertain when Cole said that, because he said it the way a man with a razor strap in his hand would tell a boy to do something.

"Aw, hell, why not," the kid said, then found the shirt and tore it into strips.

Cole sat silently on a big flat rock while the boy wrapped a crude bandage around the wound. After the boy had completed the task, Cole ordered him up onto the wagon seat. "You'll do the driving back to Fort Smith."

The rest of the men hooted, cawed at him that he was a yellow greaser to lend a hand.

"I ain't driving my ownself to no jailhouse, mister," the boy said in response to the jeers of the others.

"Well, then, I'll chain you to that tree yonder and leave you for the wolves to come and eat and get one of these other fools to do the driving."

"Hell, that's just damn' old dumb talk about wolves," the boy said. "Wolves never ate no human beings I ever heard of."

"I guess you'll find out about what wolves will or won't eat if they get the opportunity. Now climb up in that seat or go on over to that tree!"

The boy's uncertain gray eyes remained defiant a fraction longer, then he meekly climbed up onto the wagon seat and took the reins in hand.

Cole felt every jolt and jiggle of the wagon and he felt the scorn of the men and that of the boy as they rode back to Fort Smith. But none of that bothered him half as much as what he had on his mind. What he had on his mind was a woman named Anna Rain. She was Cherokee and her daddy was one of those wealthy Cherokees who owned a lot of land and was held in high standing among his own people. Cole had met Anna on one of his many forays into the Nations looking for outlaws and they both knew at first sighting that they had more than a passing interest in each other. It had progressed from there. Each time Cole crossed the Arkansas River out of Fort Smith, he made it a point to go out of his way to see her. The old man wasn't taken with the idea that his daughter loved a white man—especially a white lawman—and soon had forbidden her to see Cole again. This was what she had told Cole the last time they were together. She'd arranged to meet him in Talaquah and they'd spent the night together—their first and only time—and Cole still felt the touch of her hands and the taste of her kisses every time he thought about it.

Maybe it was having her so much on his mind that kept it off his work and had nearly got him killed. Or maybe it was because he was tired of being a lawman—which in some ways was like being a drifter in the eyes of men like Anna Rain's daddy. Maybe Cole wanted to make something more of himself so he could go to the man and lay his case out and earn his respect and his daughter's hand. But that would mean he'd have to go and make his fortune, and he sure wasn't going to make it as a deputy U.S. marshal at $50 a month and found.

So somewhere during that long hellish ride back to Fort Smith, Cole made up his mind to ride away from everything and not to look back. He'd go to Texas, raise a herd of longhorns, drive them north to Kansas. In three or four seasons he'd have a solid stake, buy a ranch, then he could come back for Anna. The only trouble with that would be that Cole never did any of those things. And the longer he was gone, the more he knew he wouldn't return. He'd come to conclude, after that first season, that Anna's daddy was right—she deserved better than John Henry Cole. But that didn't keep her from being in his heart and it didn't keep him from wanting to become a better man.

What he didn't know that day as they rode back to Fort Smith was that fifteen years later, he would be back in the Nations, brought there by a terrible twist of fate that would reveal a long-held secret—one that would come close to destroying everyone it touched. But then, if a man could see into the future, he might not want to go there.

★ ★ ★ ★ ★

Book I

★ ★ ★ ★ ★

CHAPTER ONE

Langtry, Texas
1890

Roy Bean was trimming his toenails with a paring knife and talking about hogs. "Had me two blue hogs once . . . smartest creatures God ever put on the earth, next to human beings. Though I've met plenty of human beings wasn't half as smart as them hogs, truth be told."

John Henry Cole was smoking a cigarette and watching the sun set beyond the sand hills to the west. His thoughts rambled over the last fifteen years of his life, what it had come to, the women he'd loved and lost—and maybe just a little about what lay ahead for him. He was drinking some of Roy Bean's Mexican Mustang Liniment—a greasy liquor made from the agave plant that will make you blind drunk and stupid if you get into it too heavily. It would make you think, too.

"Mind passing that jug over here, John Henry?" Roy Bean said, pausing long enough in his paring to take a hearty pull of the jug. This caused him to smack his lips and slap a palm flat atop his knee and let out a grunt. He was a rotund man with a thick nest of gray beard that he'd let grow to the length of the second button on his vest. And he was never without his tall-crowned straw sombrero held in place by a leather stampede string against wind, rain, and the vagaries of west Texas weather. He reminded Cole of a fellow he'd read about in a book given him as a gift, *Don Quixote,* a sort of wild and wondrous man who saw everything different than most people. He had an alert and mysterious gaze so you never quite knew what the man was thinking, or why he was thinking what he was.

"Them hogs of mine could swim, too," he said. "You ever seen a hog swim?"

Cole allowed as he had.

"Then you know how good they can swim. Now, for my money, you can't beat a hog as a pet. They're highly intelligent, can swim good, keep themselves clean, and, worst comes to worst, you can eat them. Something you can't do with a dog, unless you're a Comanche."

A homeless Mexican youth who had three weeks earlier drifted into the settlements of Langtry lazed on the porch. All of Roy Bean's deputies had been killed by Gypsy Davy and the boy had said he was hungry and willing to work, so Roy Bean deputized him. When Judge Bean asked him, he guessed he was maybe fifteen.

"Fifteen's old enough to start becoming a man," Bean had intoned.

Until then, Cole had been the judge's only gun, mostly because Cole hadn't made new plans as yet and because he felt sympathy for Bean. The youth's name was Armando Ortega and he was slender and quick to learn and even spoke some English that, he said, his mother's *Yanqui* lover had taught him. When Roy Bean had questioned the boy about his mother, Armando had said that she was a prostitute in Nuevo Laredo and that her *Yanqui* was an outlaw from Arizona. He had also said he didn't much care for the man who beat him often and that is why he ran away to Del Norte, and that he wanted to become a *buscador.*

"You mean a bounty hunter?" Bean had said.

"*Sí.* To hunt men like my mother's *Yanqui.*"

"Oh, well, then," Bean had said, "I reckon you come to the right place to learn how. See that lanky cuss sitting there, watching the sun come up and go down? He's an expert at hunting men."

Cole had turned a narrow eye toward Roy Bean when he had said that. Then Bean had fed the boy and given him a place to sleep on the front porch and told him he could stay for as long as he wanted just as long as he was willing to work for his keep, which the boy had been eager to agree to do.

Now Armando sat listening to Roy Bean talk about his blue hogs, and when Bean spoke of how they were good to eat, the boy said: "*¿Realmente los has comido usted?*"

"Well, I only ended up having to eat one of them back when times got hard, and having a pig that is smart and can swim don't cut much ice when a man is starving. Dang' shame, though. Buster, the other one, was never the same after that. Sorta moped about all the time. Finally sold him to a Mormon with six kids."

The boy seemed slightly distressed at the story and Bean said he could go inside and take a stick of hard candy out of the jar.

"That youngster might make a fine young gentleman someday," Bean said once Armando disappeared inside Bean's combination courthouse, saloon, general store, and apartment. "Long as he don't get in with the wrong crowd like some of them snotnoses what hang out over in Vinegaroon. Give a boy like that a pistol and a bad attitude and you end up with another John Wesley Hardin. Just what this dang' country needs . . . more John Wesley Hardins!"

They sat there for a time, passing the jug back and forth, Bean doing trim work on his toes, Armando savoring the stick of hard candy, Cole smoking, listening to night descend—the croak of frogs in the canebrakes near the river, the buzz of horseflies, the silence of settling dust.

Then they saw old Julio Valdez riding his donkey up from the tent town of Vinegaroon, one of three burgs that made up Langtry.

"Here comes the mail," Bean said, looking toward the narrow road.

Julio rode through a haze of golden dust, like some lost deity from some ancient city.

"That man gets any later with today's mail, it'll be tomorrow's mail," Bean said, wiping the corner of his mouth with a knuckle.

It took another five minutes before Julio rode his tired-looking donkey up to the Jersey Lily.

"*Hola, Señor* Bean," Julio said, seemingly as tired as the donkey.

"Step down, *compadre,* and have a taste of some good firewater. It'll put some heat in those old bones of yours," Bean said.

"*Sí,* gladly, *señor.*"

"Armando," Bean directed, "go help Julio off his donkey."

The boy stepped up quickly and gave the old man a hand for which he acted grateful and patted Armando atop his head, calling him a good lad.

"I brought you some mail," Julio said, opening a leather pouch strapped about his chest and taking from it several envelopes.

"And one for you too, *Señor* Cole," he said, handing Cole a letter.

Cole opened it while Bean and Julio sat on the porch and shared the agave liquor, which also gave Bean the opportunity to challenge the old man to a game of dominoes.

The contents of the envelope addressed to Cole were brief:

John Henry Cole. Deputy, I request your appearance in my court at your earliest convenience, but not later than thirty days from receipt of this missive.

Signed:
The Honorable Isaac Parker,
Federal Judge,
Court of the Western District,
Fort Smith, Arkansas

Cole read it a second time, then folded it, and put it in his shirt pocket. It had been a long time since he had last been in Judge Parker's courtroom and a long time since he'd been a United States deputy marshal for him. It seemed odd that Parker would still refer to Cole that way. How he'd located Cole, or what he wanted, Cole hadn't a clue. But Cole wasn't inclined to saddle the first horse in the corral and go riding to Fort Smith. Still, the mention of the place raised memories of Anna Rain and the place he still had in his heart for her after all these years.

Cole knew that a man like Parker wasn't one to make idle requests. Whatever he had in mind was serious business and Cole knew he ought to give it serious consideration. Moreover, the request was a disturbing one, like the wind is disturbing when it comes down from the mountains with the first hint of winter, or like the scent of perfume and sweat on a lonely night in the arms of a woman is disturbing. Later, Cole took out the letter and read it again, then walked out to the corral where the horses leaned against each other.

Armando brought him a tin cup of *pulque*, the agave liquor, and said: "*Señor* Bean say to bring you this."

Cole took it from him and looked into his eyes and saw innocence.

"Why do you want to hunt men, Armando?" Cole said.

His eagerness to please turned to confusion. "*¿Aqui?*"

"I mean, I heard what you said about your mamma's lover, but it seems to me it would take more than that to make you want to hunt men for a living."

Still he didn't seem fully to understand Cole's question so Cole asked him in Spanish, and he shook his head and said: *"Yo no pienso que es una cosa mala para cazar a hombres malos."*

He may have thought it was not a bad thing to chase after bad guys, but he was like all young men who had not yet tasted blood but thought they had a desire for it. Cole told him that it was true that everyone had to do something and that hunting down bad men was probably just as good and honorable a thing to do as anything, but it took a certain kind of man to be a manhunter.

Armando said he understood and that he thought he could be such a man.

"Do you also understand that men who hunt sometimes become the hunted?" Cole asked.

"Sí. I know it is true, *Señor* Cole."

"It's not glory, boy, not even close," Cole said. This again drew a confused look. It was like talking to the wind. Maybe the boy would find his place in the world, maybe not. Maybe he would become a manhunter. Or maybe he'd end up dead and forgotten, buried in a simple grave, wrapped up in a horse blanket, his mother never knowing his fate, just like so many young men who'd traveled the same bitter trail before him. Cole didn't think it was his place to be a moral guide for the young and lost, but it was hard to think about a kid dying before he got a chance to see what being a man is all about. "You ever kill one living thing?" he asked.

Armando shook his head.

"It's not what you think it is. Not even close, kid." Then Cole walked to the tent he had staked down by the river and packed his saddlebags and gave one last look around before going back up to the corral and throwing a saddle on the piebald gelding that pricked up its ears at his approach, as though it knew and understood the need to leave this place.

Roy Bean saw Cole and stood on the edge of the porch and said: "You heading out?"

"I reckon."

"Something I do to upset you?"

"No."

"You leave, I'll be back to no deputies. 'Cept Armando."

"Someone will come along who needs a job."

"Not if they heard Gypsy Davy killed all my previous deputies."

"He's dead, remember?"

"Oh, yeah, but that don't remove the taint."

"Someone will hear and not care as long as you're offering cash wages. There's always a man with a gun who's willing to use it for money."

"I reckon that's true."

Cole stepped into leather and turned the horse's head toward the east road.

"You get back this way, you'll still have a job if you want it," Bean said.

The folded letter in Cole's shirt pocket felt heavy with regret. "Judge . . . ," he said, pulling the horse up short.

"What?"

Cole wanted to tell him something about the boy, Armando, started to tell him to give him good counsel and not let him turn into a manhunter or go astray, then thought better of it. "Nothing," he said.

Bean hitched his pants and stood there, watching Cole, the bulk of his belly hanging over his belt, his trousers tucked down inside his boots, that big sombrero perched like a sand hill atop his head. *"Adiós, hombre,"* he cawed.

Cole didn't look back, and rode until darkness overtook him, until the night sky was flung with stars and the moon looked like it was waiting for him at the end of the road. It was that kind of night, peaceful and undisturbed and full of darkness. Just like a grave.

CHAPTER TWO

The old bandit saw the riders—he counted five—in the distant haze. Knew they were trouble—on the dodge. Could tell by the way they rode—weary, heads down, sleeping in the saddle—he'd done it himself a hundred times. His name was Pablo Juárez. In the old days, he had been the most feared bandit along the Río Grande. They called him *El jinete de la muerte*—The Death Rider. But time had faded those days so that they seemed more like a dream or the memory of another man's life, not his own. It was as though *El jinete de la muerte* was a man he had heard about, someone else who had done those terrible things so long ago. Nowadays he was simply an old man whose strength had left him, whose bones had become brittle, whose hands sometimes shook. But his eyes were still good to him; he could see a long distance. His heart quickened at the sight of them. He dropped the foot of the horse he'd been shoeing and straightened against the stiffness in his back. There was no mistaking it; the riders were coming to his place.

He walked to the house, called to the woman inside. She appeared in the doorway, round and plump and brown-skinned, her black hair cut straight across her wide forehead, her eyes small and black. She had once been young and pretty when he had first seen her at a *baile* in Palomas. Slender as a reed. By then, he was already a famous man, his name spoken all up and down the border. Everyone was afraid of him except this dark-eyed Indian girl who only smiled at him shyly. So he took her with him.

He spoke to her now. Told her about the riders that were coming. Told her to get some food ready. Weary men were hungry men. Feed a man until his belly is full and he might not kill you. Deny him comfort and there is no telling what he might do. That much Pablo Juárez knew from his old days. Few men came this far into what the *gringos* called No Man's Land. At least few honest men came.

He walked to the shed and stuck his hand down in the grain bin and felt around in the depth until his fingers touched the burlap wrapped around the pistol. He pulled it free and unwrapped the cloth and blew out the grain dust from the working parts and made sure every chamber had a bullet in it before rewrapping it and returning it to its hiding spot. Then he walked back out into the sunlight and waited for the riders.

When they halted, he saw one of them was a white man and the other four were Indians. They had eyes like hungry wolves. This caused a little uneasiness to rattle around in him. Still, he welcomed them and offered that they step down and water their horses.

"Your horses look tired," he said.

"Yes, we've ridden a long way," the white man said.

"I have told my wife to prepare something to eat. I saw you coming 'way off down the road there."

The white man turned halfway around in his saddle as though to look back at the road where they'd come from. "You must have pretty good eyes," he said, "the way that sun's angling."

"*Sí*, I can see pretty good still," Pablo said. The others simply sat staring at him with their wolf-hungry eyes. He still acted as though everything was OK with him and that they were more than welcome.

The white man told the others to stretch their legs and water the horses and handed his reins to one of the Indians, who offered him a bitter look in return, but he then took the horse along with his own to the tank and stood there while it drank.

The white man squatted on his heels and took some tobacco from his pocket and rolled himself a cigarette, glancing now and then back toward the Indians before saying: "Those boys are woolly as last winter's sheep."

"I'll check in the house to see how long my woman will be in fixing some supper," Pablo said. The white man nodded, looked over his shoulder, and Pablo could see that he was also taking in the lay of the place, the corral with the good horses, the house itself.

Pablo walked inside the house and asked the woman how long she'd be before she had the food ready for them and she said it would only be a few minutes. He could smell the beans cooking in the pot and the warm tortillas. He told her that when she was ready to serve them to let him know and he would come and carry out the food to them and that she was to stay inside the house until they'd left.

She asked him if everything was all right and he said: "Yes, I think it will be all right. They will just eat and rest a little, then probably go on their way."

When he came out of the house again, the Indians were all squatting on their heels in a small circle and they looked up at once at his approach.

"The food will be ready in a few minutes," he said.

"See you got some good horses there," the white man said, pointing with his nose toward the corral.

Pablo told them that his horses were all mustangs and that he'd caught them out on the bench land and had broken them to a saddle, but that they were still a little green. He told them: "It is hard to take the wild country out of a horse once he has tasted freedom. It is like a fire in their brains."

27

"Mustangs, huh?" the white man said.

"*Sí.*"

The man sniffed the air and continued to smoke his cigarette and look around.

Then Pablo heard the woman call his name and he went back inside the house and came out again, carrying the big black pot of beans and a stack of tortillas wrapped in some cheesecloth. He set the pot in the center of their circle and handed the white man the cloth of tortillas.

The man didn't say anything, simply took the cloth and separated himself one of the tortillas, and passed the rest to the Indian squatting next to him. Pablo went back inside the house and came out again with some wooden bowls and some spoons and these he handed to them and watched as they filled the bowls with beans and ate greedily, their spoons clattering against the bowls.

He told them they could stay and rest as long as they wanted and that he would be inside if they needed anything, but it seemed they hardly even heard him, so engrossed in their hunger as they were. He turned and started to walk toward the shed when the white man called: "I thought you said you were going to the house?" Pablo answered, yes, that he was but first he had to check on something. His heart was pounding hard. He had a bad feeling about these *proscritos* and he knew that he had to be prepared for the worst.

His hand sought out the pistol in the grain bin and this time, when he withdrew it, he felt the presence of someone in the shed. Turning, he saw the shadow of one of the Indians, then saw the flash of dying sunlight touch the barrel of the Indian's gun as he stepped out of the shadows and said: "What the hell are you going to do with that, old man?"

The sacking was still wrapped around his pistol, tied with a string. Then something snapped hard against his head and caused red light to flash behind his eyes.

Pablo awoke to the chill of night air and his arms ached, and, when he tried to move, he found that he was tied to one of the blackjack fence posts of the corral, his arms trussed with wire and pulled up sharply behind him. A strand of wire encircled his chest and his legs were stretched out before him and he could not move or stand. Something sticky melded one eye closed. With his other eye he saw the sky overhead was black as velvet and flung with stars and in the distance he could hear the call of coyotes.

He blinked his stuck eye trying to free it and eventually he did but that side of his head was painful and he had to bite the inside of his cheek to keep from crying out. He could see now the yellow squares of light from the house and he listened, trying to hear what was going on in there but he heard nothing. He cursed his luck and himself for not having been alert enough and letting the Indian get the drop on him. For a long time he watched the yellow squares of light, and then sometime in the night they went out.

Next he knew, the dawn had risen, gray and chill, and he heard the disturbance of horses there in the corral and saw that the Indians and the white man were saddling his horses and leading their own by ropes out of the corral and toward the road. When one of them turned and looked back at him, he pretended to be unconscious but saw them through the narrow slits of his eyes. The one looking back was the young one among them—just a boy not more than fourteen or fifteen.

All that day he sat there helpless, calling as best as he could for the woman to come and remove the wire from around him, but she never came and soon his throat was too dry to call to her and he began to fret for her.

Then when he thought he could stand it no longer, that the pain in his head and his legs and hips would cause him to go mad, the sun settled to earth and flared brightly before disappearing beyond the horizon and he prayed for death to come quickly.

Sometime that night he sensed death had come and opened his eyes and saw the face of one of the Indians, dark and bronze, in the half moonlight.

"So, you are still alive," the Indian said. He was the same one who had looked back at him that morning. The boy.

He didn't say anything. He noticed the pistol the boy wore in a scabbard and the long-bladed knife in his belt.

The boy looked into his eyes for a moment, then worked the wire free by twisting loose its ends. Once he'd finished, he started to say something, then fell silent.

Pablo's weakness caused him to topple over. Unable to feel his arms or legs, unable to sit upright, he lay there, tasting dust in his mouth. He watched as the Indian boy mounted his pony and rode off. After several minutes the feeling came back into his limbs—a dull heaviness that soon began to prickle his blood and he began crawling toward the house. *Like a child*, he thought, *like a* chico, *small and helpless.*

By the time he reached the porch of the house, he was able to stand a little and it took nearly all of his energy to do so. He entered the house and found her lying on her back there in the middle of the floor and at this sight he fell to his knees next to her and wept. She was as cold and lifeless as the earth and they had done terrible things to her. He pulled a blanket from the bed and covered them both with it and he lay next to her all that night, weeping, and eventually fell into a fitful sleep.

The next morning he made a small meal, enough to give him some strength, and, once finished, he went out to the shed and found a shovel and began to dig a grave for her. It took all that day to dig a proper grave, and when he finished, he sat heavily on the mound of dirt and wept some more.

Then he buried her and the next morning he set fire to the house and began walking down the road that led away from the house, the last of his life carried on a wind of fire, but he did not look back. He had no gun, no horse, nothing but the clothes he wore, the frayed straw sombrero, and a hatred like flames burning in his soul. Thus he went in search of them.

Chapter Three

The judge was standing at the windows with his back to him when John Henry Cole entered his chambers. The windows were partly raised to let in fresh air. The judge's gaze was fixed on the unfolding drama taking place in the courtyard below. There was the scent of rain.

The chamber was cavernous. The furnishings consisted of a large polished oak desk, three chairs, and on the opposite wall was the judge's prized cherub clock that he'd purchased in France. It was fashioned with a pair of gilt cherubs riding a chariot with prancing stallions surrounding the clock's porcelain face. It rested on a marble base and chimed hourly. It had a solid steady tick.

The hangman, George Maledon, was preparing the scaffold for the Parrot brothers like a director meticulously preparing the stage for the final act of a play. Only this would be a performance that would end in death.

"We don't get this many for the opera," the judge muttered, indicating the crowd that had gathered.

Cole moved to one of the windows, his spurs sounding like loose change spilling to the floor. The judge barely seemed to notice his presence. Cole could see the deep concentration furrowing the judge's brow, the intense stare of his clear gray eyes transfixed on the scene below. Cole knew him well enough to know that this was not something Isaac Parker took pleasure in, watching his judicial decree being carried out, watching men being hanged.

It had been a long time since Cole had been in these chambers and the last time he had been, he was still nursing a bullet wound Lucky Baker's wife had put in him. He'd told the judge he was quitting and laid his badge on the desk and walked away, and they hadn't seen each other again until now. The judge hadn't changed much except for around the eyes. They looked a little more tired, as though they'd seen too much misery.

"Why do you do it, Judge?" Cole asked as he watched Maledon check and recheck the knots and lengths of his ropes. "Why do you watch?"

Without turning his attention to Cole he said in a voice that was surprisingly soft: "It is my duty to see it through to its completion, this business of justice. I owe it to the victims and, to some degree, to the condemned as well."

"Well, I wouldn't waste too much of my concerns for those boys," Cole said as he watched the deputies bring Edwin and Duvall Parrot through the doors that led up from the jail in the basement, one floor below the judge's chambers. A light rain began falling. Umbrellas mushroomed amid the crowd. Cole eased the makings from his shirt and crafted a cigarette.

The rain fell harder. The deputies led the Parrot brothers slowly across the courtyard between the parting sea of spectators and up the lumber steps of the scaffold. It was a slow, shuffling procession because of the leg irons shackled around their ankles. The irons not only kept a man from escaping, it took away his strut, made him appear weak and apt for slaughter. They were bareheaded and their scraggly hair lay pasted to their heads and down along their necks. Impossibly they looked like innocent boys, caught out in the rain, their faces dripping water. Their cheap calico shirts were pressed damply against their hunger-thin bodies. The deputies held them by the waist as they helped them awkwardly up the steps where the "Prince of Hangmen" was giving a final check to the pair of ropes he'd prepared for them.

"Still," the judge said, the soft modulation of his voice nearly lost in the room's expanse, "no matter what their crimes, they are someone's sons. Somewhere, a mother weeps for her lost children. . . ."

Cole smoked without saying anything.

George Maledon wore a suit of black, a silk necktie against a white shirt, his hair, sparse, streaked with iron strands, combed straight back away from his head in a manner that gave his countenance a fierceness in spite of his diminutive stature. Add to this the bushy brows above the deeply cavernous eyes and you had the complete picture of a man who represented death in a way and manner that lent it a formal civility.

Maledon stood respectfully, waiting for his actors to arrive, his hands resting on a brace of pistols, butts thrust forward, strapped into holsters on a wide leather belt with a large square buckle. The pistols were sentiments from his days as a policeman and deputy sheriff of Sebastian County. He had shot several men with them.

The Parrot brothers finally arrived on the platform, where the hangman stood, erect and ready, to direct them through their final act. He looked squarely into the eyes of each of the brothers. To Maledon, they were just young outlaws with bad haircuts and no more future than tick-fevered cattle—trouble the community of man did not need. But like the judge, Maledon took no real pleasure in the hanging. It was simply a matter of duty with him, like reading the Bible or going to church. He'd done it fifty-four times already; the Parrot boys would make fifty-five and fifty-six. He kept a ledger, that's how he knew, that's how he remembered each of them.

The rain fell steadily now, snapping against the black skins of the umbrellas. Puddles bubbled like hot brown soup in the muddy courtyard. A small boy stamped his feet, splaying up water until his mother shook him still.

Reverend Simms stepped forward, the brim of his Quaker hat spilling water, his hands clutching a small Bible with oxblood leather covers. He stepped first to Ed Parrot, spoke something, but Ed hardly acknowledged the gesture. Then he stepped around back of Ed and positioned himself alongside Duvall and spoke something to him. Even from where Cole stood, he could see something visible travel the length of Duvall's body, and Maledon stepped quickly forward and settled a hand under the boy's elbow and steadied him.

"Buck up, son, it won't be long now. I know my work. It won't even hurt. The rope'll break your neck bone and it'll just feel like nothing at all."

"How would you know?" Duvall cried out.

The judge closed his eyes for a moment. Cole blew a stream of smoke against the glass, watched it curl up and fold into a blue cloud. Hanging was an ugly business. Even if it was done under sanction of the courts, it was still an ugly business.

Maledon looped the hemp ropes around the necks of each of the Parrot brothers, then with something akin to gentleness he slipped the knots down snugly, but delicately. He did it quickly, knowledgeably, and without hesitation. He'd see these boys off just like all the others. They'd die without a whimper. He prided himself in knowing his business. Then he stepped back and said—"Be brave, boys."—and shoved the trap door levers forward.

Something shuddered through the crowd when the bodies dropped through the traps and jolted to a stop at the end of Maledon's ropes. For a moment more the crowd stood with their mouths open and watched as the bodies turned three-quarters to the left, then twisted back again, and came to a full rest. The necks of the men broken, their souls fled, the crowd slowly dispersed.

The judge had opened his eyes in time to witness the event, then, before the Parrot boys stopped turning at the end of their ropes, he turned away from the window and slumped in the big leather chair behind his desk.

"John Henry," he said as though acknowledging Cole's presence for the first time.

"Judge."

Then for a long full moment he simply stared at his own hands resting atop the green blotter on his desk. "Sometimes when I think of it," he said without looking up, "I wonder if *these* hands haven't put to death more than the guns of all my deputies combined."

"You don't get them hanged, Judge," Cole said, taking a chair opposite him. "They do that to themselves."

The judge's gaze, now saturnine, lifted to meet Cole's. "I don't remember you as a man with so little compassion," he said. "Did being a lawman do that to you, or was it something else?"

It was a question Cole didn't care to answer.

The judge sighed and said: "I'm glad you could come."

Cole waited for the judge to tell him the reason he'd sent the telegram. For a long full moment he didn't speak. It was easy to guess he was still thinking about a pair of young boys, hanging from the ends of ropes. Cole noticed the way the judge looked him over and knew he didn't entirely approve of what he saw. He was a fastidious man and expected the men who worked for him to be so as well. But Cole didn't work for him and it had been a long ride from Texas, so the judge didn't mind so much that the salt-stained Stetson that rested on Cole's right knee could stand cleaning or that Cole needed a shave and a fresh change of clothes.

"I am indebted to you for coming, John Henry," Parker said. "This is a very grave matter I'm faced with."

Cole shifted in his chair.

"I've a situation before me that I would like you to handle," he said, slipping open the top right-hand drawer of his desk, from which he took several papers. "As you know, we cannot arrest Indians in the Nations unless they've committed crimes against whites. Indians committing crimes against Indians are handled by the law enforcement agencies of the various tribes, their Indian police, and the Light Horse."

Cole knew all this already. The judge laid the papers on his desk. They were Wanted posters.

"These men," he continued, "are of Indian blood, except the one who is married into the Cherokee tribe."

Cole quickly examined the posters.

"Their crimes are grievous. And they have been careful in committing their aggressions only against other Indians. They have committed murder, rape, and armed robbery. In the last ten days alone, they have cut a bloody swath from Talaquah to the far western reaches of the territory." The judge drew breath, ran fingers through his hair. "There is something else, too."

Cole watched as his gaze fell upon the posters once more. "What?" he asked.

"These men, these murderers, have made it a point to assassinate any and all Indian Police that they can find. They've killed half a dozen already."

Cole felt a throb set itself against his temples.

"This man," the judge said, picking up one of the posters and tapping his finger on the poor photographic image, "is their leader. Caddo Pierce, a white man but claims to be Cherokee by marriage. He's bad business. He has also killed two lawmen in New Mexico Territory on a foray before retreating back into the Nations. The only good news is that there is a five-thousand-dollar reward for him in New Mexico, payable to the man who brings him in."

Maybe the judge had forgotten that Pierce was the man Cole had been looking for when the Indian's woman had shot him, but Cole hadn't forgotten. "That's it, then. You thought maybe I was down on my luck and could use the money?"

Parker leaned forward, his eyes intense. "I received a telegram this morning from Jimmy Wild Bird, head of the Cherokee police force in Talaquah, asking for our help in capturing these devils."

The name of Jimmy Wild Bird stirred up more old memories that were almost as painful as the wound Lucky Baker's woman had given Cole. Jimmy Wild Bird and Cole had a connection the judge didn't know about. Maybe the judge saw something in Cole's eyes because he asked: "You know Jimmy Wild Bird?"

"By reputation," Cole said.

The judge seemed to accept that answer. "Caddo Pierce and his gang have already murdered three of Jimmy's officers," Parker said. "Murdered them and left bloody notes pinned to their chests."

Cole waited for him to tell what the notes said.

"All that Officer Wild Bird would say in regard to the notes was that it had to do with making bad medicine on the Indian police and that it included a threat to kill not only them but their families if it was found out that any of them were hunting Pierce and his bunch."

"Sounds like it's more than just a threat," Cole observed.

The judge shook his head, sighed, tapped his fingers against the poster. "Officer Wild Bird's telegram was sparsely detailed. The point is, Jimmy can't find a man in the Nations that's willing to go up against Pierce and his gang now."

"What about the Light Horse?"

"The Indian militia?" Judge Parker's features sagged. "Not

even the militia is willing to track them into No Man's Land, and that's where they've gone according to Wild Bird. And before they headed in that direction, they raped and murdered the wife of an Osage policeman, then shot him and burned their house with them still in it. Those are the last killings I've heard of."

"You want me to go and assist Jimmy Wild Bird?"

"It can't be anything official. I can't legally send a single deputy unless they commit a crime against a white man." He shook his head regretfully. "I can't even pay your fees for mileage or meals if you go."

Cole looked at the posters once more, thought about Jimmy Wild Bird, about the threats of the desperados, and about Jimmy's wife—the thing they had in common, the thing the judge didn't know about. Cole dropped the posters back on Judge Parker's desk. "A man that would go under the conditions you just laid out would have to be either a fool, or a man that didn't place much value on his life. You think I'm one or the other?"

Parker sat motionlessly, his thoughts seemingly elsewhere. Rain ran down the windows in grimy streaks. Outside, you could hear the deputies hammering the lids on the coffins of the Parrot brothers. Then, clearing his throat, the judge said in a voice edged with resolve: "It'd take a damned fool to go and help Jimmy Wild Bird, considering what he's up against, on that account you may be right. A fool, or a man just as bone-mean as Caddo Pierce and his bunch. I'm not saying you're either, but I had to ask. I had to ask it for that poor Indian policeman because they're sure going to kill him and some others before it's all said and done."

Cole rubbed a finger through the crease of his hat brim, then said: "There's something you need to know, Judge." Cole opined that maybe he already knew what Cole was about to say, but the judge nodded and said: "Go ahead, say what's on your mind."

"If I go, it won't be to bring any of them in to stand trial in the Nations."

They were both aware of how some of the tribes in the Nations viewed certain outlaws, especially Indian outlaws. In some cases, a captured man might be treated harshly, while in others, he might be allowed to go free—it was a matter of judgment not completely understood or accepted by the white federal courts.

"You know I can't condone what you're suggesting," Parker stated flatly.

"And you know the only law west of the Arkansas is the iron a man carries on his hip."

"I know that their justice is not always the same as our own," he said. "I don't necessarily agree with everything that goes on over there among the tribes, but I have no real choice in the matter. What you are referring to is premeditated murder."

"Not murder," Cole said. "It will come down to them or the man who hunts them. They won't surrender. Men like them never do."

"Then I have been wrong in asking you to come," Parker said, the disappointment clear in his voice.

"You're a decent man, Judge. I respect what you're trying to do. But, I've been to the far side of the river, and I told myself I wasn't ever going back. But that's what you're asking me to do. I can't make any promises and I won't. If it comes to me or them, I know who's going to get buried."

With that, Cole stood, then started for the door. He needed a stiff drink, maybe two.

"Hold on, sir!" Parker's voice commanded.

Cole turned, his own anger rising.

The judge said: "Perhaps my own view of the world has been limited just to these sets of windows, these chambers, this courtroom. I have not had the advantage . . . or disadvantage, if you will . . . of going into the field. It would be remiss of me to prejudge you on this matter." Parker stood up from behind his desk, turned once more to the tall windows and the rain crawling down them. For a moment he nodded his head, as though holding a silent conversation with himself. Then, without turning to face Cole, he said: "You go and help Jimmy Wild Bird bring these boys to bay. However you do it, I'll trust that justice will be served."

With that, the conversation was finished.

The rain had nearly stopped by the time Cole stepped outside the courthouse. A wagon carrying the coffins of the Parrot brothers clattered through the gate leading from the courtyard. Cole watched as the wagon rolled down the muddy street toward Potter's Field.

"Them boys' troubles are all over now," George Maledon said, appearing suddenly alongside Cole. "You hiring back on as a deputy?"

Cole shook his head.

"Just wondering," Maledon said. "Judge lost two more men last week. Maybe see you in church." He walked stiffly down the muddy street toward the nearest saloon as was his custom after a hanging.

Cole's mind was full of conflict. On the one hand he was facing going back to a world he'd vowed to leave forever, and to a woman he'd long ago thought he'd gotten over—a woman who was now married to another man. He still had strong feelings for Anna Rain, but some sorrow, too, since he'd not heard from her in a long, long time. Maybe he was wrong, maybe all the hurt and loss in his life had led him to this one point. And maybe he didn't know exactly why he'd risk his life for an uncertain future, for a woman toward whom he realized he still had strong feelings, and in a place that had nearly killed him once already.

Cole tried to find the answers in a bottle of Tennessee sipping whiskey that evening, but all he found were more questions. He could either ride away, or perhaps he could maybe find peace at last. Whatever he'd been doing these last fifteen years didn't seem to be working. He knew he wanted to see Anna again, if for no other reason than to close that door between them. And he knew her life was in some real danger according to what the judge had told him. In the end, he knew he could not just ride away from the ghosts of his past. He had to ride back to meet them.

CHAPTER FOUR

Time shifts sometimes even when you're standing still. John Henry Cole had offers that night from the prostitutes who plied their trade in the Big Muddy. Some were comely, some were not. But none even came close to taking his mind off Anna, the assignment the judge wanted him to take on, or the fact that in the last twenty years he hadn't made much of himself in the way that most would call success. He knew horses and guns and cattle. He even thought he knew a little about women. But beyond that, he couldn't show much to prove he was anything more than a drifter.

Going back into the Nations after the renegades, he knew he'd need help. He did a little checking around and learned that another old name from the past was in the area—Joe Digger. Cole was told that he kept a camp outside of Fort Smith near the banks of the Arkansas. Digger was a posse man—a gun for hire that Fort Smith deputies sometimes used. He was a taciturn Tennessean who kept to himself, a man of mystery, but also a man of wide reputation for collecting bounties on wanted men. Cole rode out to Digger's camp after his meeting with Judge Parker and two whiskies.

Joe Digger's camp was nothing more than a large canvas tent surrounded by a growing pile of rusty tin cans. Two horses were picketed nearby and a wood fire crackled in a circle of rocks.

Cole reined in and helloed the camp. Joe Digger stepped through the tent's flaps.

"John Henry Cole," the bounty hunter said after a moment of staring at Cole. His voice was as lurking as a shadow, full of distrust and caution. "I heard you got killed by a Mexican bandit down along the Río."

"Sorry to disappoint you," Cole said. "You mind if I get down so we can talk?"

Digger nodded, and Cole dismounted.

Digger's gaze followed Cole's every move. He wore a Walker Colt on one hip and a butcher knife on the other. He was all bone and pale blue flesh and hollow-eyed like he'd been living in a cave for a long time. The skin around his eyes was creased with black grime, as was the wattle of his neck below the wiry beard. Dirt and gun oil caked the knuckles of his hands and under his fingernails.

"I'll get straight to it," Cole said.

Digger blinked but said nothing.

"I need a man to go over into the Nations with me."

"How much?"

"Nothing up front, maybe some reward money at the end."

"*Maybe* some reward money?"

Cole realized that it wasn't going to be easy to convince him to go into the Nations on the speculation there might be some reward money in it. "Nothing up front," he repeated.

Digger grunted.

"One of the men I'm after has a reward posted on him down in New Mexico Territory. Five thousand, if we find him. And if we do find him, you can take him back to Santa Fe."

"How come them New Mexican peace officers don't collect him up?"

"One man's a lot to look for if you don't know where he is."

Digger looked off to something in the distance, spat, brought his gaze back to Cole. "Twenty-five hunnered, split two ways," he said doubtfully.

"I'm not interested in the reward. We catch him, you keep the reward."

"What's your interest, then?" he said, eyeing Cole with suspicion.

"It's personal."

"Shit." The bounty hunter looked off again.

Cole looked around the squalid camp, then said: "I can see where leaving a swell place like this to go after *maybe* five thousand dollars in reward money would be a hell of a decision." That bit of sarcasm was lost on Digger, a man bereft of humor. "There's five of them," Cole added. "Four Creek renegade boys besides the white man with the reward on him . . . killers every one. Thought you ought to know." Cole turned and put a foot in the stirrup, then swung up into the saddle. "We catch up with them, you can have whatever horses and weapons we recover for your troubles as well."

Cole turned the piebald's head back toward the road to Fort Smith, paused, then said: "I'll be leaving first light tomorrow. You decide to come, meet me at the ferry." Then, without any hope whatsoever that he'd sold Digger on the idea, he rode back to Fort Smith.

Once there, Cole's first stop was the hardware store where he bought boxes of ammunition for his Winchester rifle, the Peacemaker, and the Colt Lightning hide-out gun he wore in a shoulder rig. Afterward, he stopped at the mercantile, wrote out a list of supplies he'd need, and handed it to the clerk, telling him he'd return for them. Then he stopped off at the livery stable and told the old man there he'd need to rent a pack horse for two, maybe three weeks.

"And put a new set of shoes on the General," he instructed, handing the reins of the chesty gelding over to the smithy. "A little extra grain in his feed as well."

He visited the bathhouse, soaked for an hour in a tub of hot water, shaved, sipped whiskey. Then he picked up his supplies and took them with him to a boarding house for the night.

At dawn the next morning, Cole rolled up his sougans and packed his saddlebags with the supplies. Then he walked the General, along with the pack horse he'd rented, up the plank of the ferry. The sky to the west of the river was smudged with thin gray clouds. The waters of the Arkansas were gun-metal gray under the early light. The wind blew sharply across the river, chopping up small waves that lapped against the sides of the boat.

Cole made a cigarette and smoked it as he waited for the ferryman to finish the loading of supplies, men, and horses going across to the other side. He had a dark feeling that this time he might not come out of the Nations alive. He didn't know what it was exactly, just a feeling that flowed through his veins like the cold, uninviting water of the Arkansas this morning. Whatever the risks, he knew they were worth it if he could see Anna Rain again, if he could possibly save her, even if it meant saving the man she was married to as well. He took a last draw of the shuck, flipped it overboard, and watched it drown in a hiss.

"You still offerin' that *maybe* reward money?"

Cole turned and saw Joe Digger walking his horses up the plank onto the ferry. "I am."

"Then let's go kill a few of them sons-a-bitches."

CHAPTER FIVE

The sound of the pistols broke through her sleep. Dawn and cold crept into the room like unwanted guests. She slipped from the blankets, reached for the cotton shift draped over a chair, and drew it over her head, the length of it spilling down her dark, lithe body.

She crossed the room of the small cabin, moved to the window, looked through the cheaply made glass panes, and saw Jimmy standing out in the side yard. Jimmy was firing his pistols at a row of peach cans atop a weathered plank. The sharp crack of the revolvers reverberated against the walls of the cabin. Jimmy stood in a cloud of blue gunsmoke—his face grim, determined, his eyes intense beneath the brim of his black felt hat. He fired the pistols alternately, first one, then the other, each time lifting them straight out in front of him, then slowly thumbing back the hammer before squeezing the trigger.

Each time he fired the pistols, the sound caused her body to jerk as if someone had slapped her. She turned away from the window, set about making coffee—a blend of Arbuckle, chicory, and wild mint leaves. She built a fire in the iron stove. The stove was trimmed in nickel and had porcelain handles on the oven door. Jimmy had ordered it through a catalogue and he and two other men had taken a wagon to Talaquah to pick it up when it arrived from St. Louis in order to deliver it to her on Christmas day. This was before the trouble started.

She took a pan of dabber biscuits she'd made the day before

and set them on the table along with a small jar of fresh honey and waited for the coffee to finish brewing. The stove's fire chased the chill out of the room and she could smell the sweetness of the burning wood. The days seemed to run together of late. Jimmy up every morning before dawn, firing his pistols at peach cans until the barrels grew too hot to touch, until her ears rang. When he wasn't firing the pistols or cleaning them, or looking at the Wanted posters of the five men in brooding silence, he spent his time moping around the house or outside in the yard. A man lost within himself, it seemed.

She'd thought at first it was just the killings of Leo Bennet and Rafe Adel and Willy Palmer that caused his brooding. But then she remembered Jimmy had been slowly sinking into himself for a long time before the killings. She stood, crossed the room, and picked up a small hand mirror that was lying on a stand next to the bed. The mirror was encased in bone, the edges of the glass black.

She held it in front of her, studied the face, oval as a teardrop, the dark eyes lost now of their innocence, the full mouth, the cinnamon skin that was without flaw, but without its former beauty. *When had she grown so plain?* She ran fingers through the straight, glossy hair that hung to her waist. Tipping the mirror slightly, she could see the soft swell of her small firm breasts jutting against the cotton material of the shift. She touched one of them lightly through the gown; a sharp tingle of forbidden pleasure caused her to take the hand away quickly.

It had been a long time since Jimmy had touched her breasts. But she was not sure she cared any longer. His moroseness seemed to have spilled over to her and taken away any pleasure she once had. She placed the mirror face down, went back to the stove, poured herself a cup of coffee, and sat at the table.

When had they ceased being man and wife and become more like brother and sister? she wondered, her lips tentative in sipping the coffee, the steam rising against her cheeks. She tried to place a time on when she first came to realize that she no longer loved the man who stood outside her door, shooting his pistols. Tried to define when was the first time she realized how she stopped looking forward to the nights with him in her bed. And when had he become simply a man whose clothes she washed, whose meals she cooked, whose absence had become more welcome than his presence? They were questions without answers, like people without shadows.

Thinking about it caused her hands to tremble slightly. She set the cup down, pressed her palms together as if in prayer. She closed her eyes against the quiet heat of the guilt that had lately come to her unbidden when she thought of leaving him, of finding her happiness again. Her guilt increased whenever she thought of the only other man she'd ever loved.

The door suddenly rattled open on its leather hinges. Jimmy stood framed in a quadrangle of light, his features obscured. He stepped in, closed the door behind him. He smelled of gun oil and cordite and sweat. He was wearing the pistols in his belt, their long barrels down along his legs.

He was squarely built, broad strong shoulders, thick chest, arms heavily muscled. His black hair was cropped short, cut straight across his forehead, adding a bluntness to his features. He had thin wispy mustaches—something he emulated from the white lawmen who wore them almost like black threads of silk. It was said that Indians could not grow face hair, just like they could not drink whiskey without going crazy. Lots of things were said about Indians, mostly by white people and most of them untrue and unflattering.

Without greeting, he went to the stove, reached above it on a shelf, took down a tin cup, and poured himself some of the coffee. He smelled it first before sipping it as he usually did. She watched his face. It showed no expression to indicate his feelings or his mood about either her coffee, or her presence.

He sat at the table opposite her, reached for the pan of biscuits, took one, broke it apart, spread some honey on it, then stuck it in his mouth, the honey running down his fingers. She watched as he ate and licked his fingers, wondering if he could taste the gun oil mixed in with the honey, wondering how that would taste.

She remained silent as he ate. His eyes flicked upward several times from his concentration on the honey-sopped biscuits. His gaze was like the flight of a butterfly, darting, landing on her, then darting away again, never staying on her for very long at a time. She could hear the soles of his boots scraping the rungs of the chair as he ate; it was a habit of his to put his feet on the rungs, like smelling the coffee before he drank it.

Nearly twelve years of marriage and she had learned everything there was to know about him. The way he could walk around in the dark without stumbling over things, the way his breathing sounded in his sleep. She had learned the sounds of him, his scent, and anticipated what he was going to say before he said it. There was only one thing she did not know about him. The only thing she didn't understand, couldn't fathom was the darkness in him. It was like death, this darkness, an unknowable thing. Beyond that one thing, it troubled her to think that she knew everything about him. She wished that there could still be secrets to him, small surprises that would keep her tied to him in spite of his darkness. But Jimmy had never been a man to hide anything about himself except for this one thing. Plain and simple in his outlook on life, his beliefs steady, unchanging, his habits open. He lacked guile. When he spoke, he said what he meant. When he took on a job, he became a slave to it.

Every morning he rose and went to the privy at the same time. He ate his meals at the same time. He went to bed at the same time and got up at the same time. He even brushed his horses the same way—right side first, then left. He had become as predictable as the rain in spring and the cold in winter. She regretted knowing so much about him. And now the only thing she did not know about him, she could not know.

He ate three of the biscuits and poured himself a second cup of coffee. She watched him lick his fingers over and over, then sip more of the coffee.

"I am going to Talaquah, Anna," he said, his voice flat, void of emotion. "I am going to see if Judge Parker has sent me any word about maybe sending some deputies over here to help me."

"Oh."

Every few days he had made the ten-mile trip into Talaquah, hoping to find a telegram from the white judge in Fort Smith. She had enjoyed the days when he was gone, their lovely silence. But now she was feeling the need for the company of others, of someone who did not exact anything from her. She wanted to visit her cousin, Rudina, perhaps shop at the mercantile. The prospect of this caused her spirits to rise.

"I will go with you," she said.

His gaze flitted to meet hers. "Why?" he asked.

"There are things I need," she said. And when he did not ask her what things she needed, she listed them: "Flour, sugar, salt. Some red thread. I would like to see Rudina. I'd like to see Bone, too."

"Oh."

His gaze floated away, lowered, rose, shifted this way and that. "I'm hoping the judge will send someone," he said.

"You will only be murdered yourself if you go after those Creeks," she said.

He didn't say anything. His features grew sullen, as though he were a child she had reprimanded.

"It's true," she said. "If those men know that you are after them, they will kill you like they did Leo and Rafe and Willy and all those others."

"I got to find them," he said. "It's my job."

For forty dollars a month and some fine money? she thought. She reserved the criticism of his dogged devotion to a job that paid him so little, offered him so little, but demanded so much. How could she hope to understand what made him risk his life for basically nothing? She would not allow herself openly to criticize him. Though she was not in love with him, she would not show him disrespect. It was the only thing that bound her to him, the respect she held for him as her husband. But even the thread of respect was fraying.

"I just don't see why you have to give your life when everyone else is afraid to help. You're just one man, Jimmy."

"Maybe the deputies will come," he said.

She remembered Willy Palmer, Jimmy's best friend and deputy and the first one to die. She remembered most about him his loud laughter that could fill a room. Willy had been part Cherokee, part Seminole. He had had a wife and four children. He used to ride the children on his shoulders and cause them to laugh like he did. Sometimes, when he would come for Jimmy and Jimmy was not home, Willy would sit in the kitchen with her and drink her chicory coffee and say: "My, my, that's some good coffee, sister." He would regale her with funny stories and was good company on lonely wet days when Jimmy was gone. She missed Willy more than she missed Leo and Rafe.

If they killed Jimmy, she wondered if she would miss him as much as she missed Willy. She wondered how terrible she'd feel if Jimmy died, what form of emptiness would it bring her that she didn't already possess?

"I will go to Talaquah with you," she said again.

He seemed to suffer her determination. She wondered at

times why he never let his anger spill over onto her. She had once seen him beat a man nearly to death—a prisoner that had tried to grab his gun. Only the intervention of Willy and Rafe saved the man's life. There was plenty of testimony to his brutal resolve as a policeman. He was not a man to fool with, the Cherokees said. She had no doubt that Jimmy could and did boil to brutal violence when it was called for. But he never once raised a hand to her. She knew he never would. It was just one more of the things she knew about him.

"Anna, it's . . . ," he started to protest, but then his gaze darted away again, carrying with it his words. "I'll go and saddle the horses," he said then. He stood and walked outside.

She was at once glad to be going to Talaquah and disappointed that Jimmy hadn't said what he had started to say in protest of her going. It was just another aspect of her frustration with him, his willingness to live life around her. The killings had done something to him inside. They had damaged his pride at being a good policeman. Rafe and Willy and Leo had been close friends, but it wasn't the loss of their friendship that gnawed at the guts of Jimmy as much as it was his damaged pride. Of that much she was certain.

He had let his men be murdered, that's the way he thought of it. He had not been a good enough policeman to stop five ragged renegades from killing decent men like Rafe and Willy and Leo. Men with families. Men of honor. Their bodies had been brought home in the back of a wagon under tarps slick with rain. All their goodness and all their decency and honor had not saved them. And neither had Jimmy. That's how he saw it.

When Rafe and Leo and Willy were killed, she'd tried coming to him, tried drawing him into her, tried being intimate with him as she had done before things between them had grown cold and distant. For in spite of everything, she felt deep compassion for his loss and the loss of his honor. At one point, Jimmy had laid his head against her and wept, his tears dropping onto her breasts. But when she tried to comfort him by speaking to him in a way that a wife speaks to her husband about sorrowful matters of the heart, he withdrew and became silent about the incident and would never speak of it beyond that time. After that he no longer touched her, except for the times when he would rut against her in the darkness, his damage spilling out of him, it seemed, and into her. It was only in those times that she truly disliked him.

She stood, went to the window, and watched as he saddled the horses. She wondered how many days were left to them. It was a thought risen from the bone.

CHAPTER SIX

Joe Digger was very drunk by the time they hit the outskirts of Talaquah late the third evening. Digger had been tugging at a bottle of mash whiskey—one of several he had among his packs—since the noon hour. Cole wasn't pleased about Diggers's behavior, but he wasn't paying the man a cent to come along and therefore couldn't order him to stop the drinking. The only thing such an attempt might accomplish would be Diggers's indignant departure from the scene, something Cole felt he could ill afford. But he did make up his mind that once they got on the heels of the renegades he'd demand that the man stay sober. Cole wasn't about to get killed because he had a drunkard watching his back.

Joe Digger talked to himself in his drunkenness, cursed and muttered names: "Pa's comin' for ya, Taddy . . . take ya outta that cold dark grave yer lyin' in! Hold on, boy, hold on. . . ."

Cole knew as well as anyone that uncorking the bottle was the quickest way to set the demons loose in a man's soul. He didn't care to guess what demons Joe Digger had unleashed on himself—he had plenty of his own to wrestle with. By the time they arrived in Talaquah, it was nearly midnight.

"We'll stay the night and go see Jimmy Wild Bird first thing in the morning," Cole said as they reined in at a livery.

Cole wasn't sure whether or not Digger had heard, or if he even understood. He tried to dismount, fell, landed on his back in the street, one foot still in the stirrup. Cole helped him to his feet, led him inside the livery, found an empty stall, and dropped him into it on a pile of horse-scented straw.

"Sleep it off, Digger. I'll be back for you in the morning."

He was already snoring by the time Cole unsaddled their horses, filled the troughs with grain, and pitched some hay into the stalls. Then he hefted the Winchester rifle and walked outside and down to where the lights of town glowed in the windows of the saloons and hurdy-gurdies. Cole knew of a hotel not far up the street if it hadn't burned down or gone bust. He remembered it as a modest, one-story hotel that had clean comfortable rooms and was owned by a Cherokee named Sam Littlefinger. The other reason he remembered it was because Anna and he had stayed there that time, just a week before he had been shot by Lucky Baker's woman.

Cole was weary and his head was buzzing like it was full of bees and he was glad to see the hotel was still in operation. He rapped on the door until a light came on and a man who wasn't Sam Littlefinger answered in his underdrawers. He had a sleepy look behind the flare of a bull's-eye lantern. Cole asked for and got the same room Anna and he had had.

He dropped his saddlebags on a chair, rested his rifle in a corner, and sank to the bed almost too tired to pull off his boots. He pressed his face to the pillows. He lay there, remembering how it was when she had been there with him. He remembered most her scent—like the air after lightning and rain. Over the years he'd tried to keep track of her, heard she'd married Jimmy Wild Bird, a man Cole knew only slightly—but like her a Cherokee, someone her daddy would approve of, a man of his own race. Cole was still thinking about her when he fell asleep.

In the morning, Cole found Joe Digger already up, checking the forelegs of his horse. He was as sober as a deacon on Sunday and showed no effects from the previous evening's binge, except for being crabby.

"Left me in a god-damn' stable," he muttered when Cole approached him. "Woke up, my back was sore, smelled like horseshit, and had straw in my mouth. That any way to treat a man?"

"You were drunk," Cole said. "You fell off your horse. I could have left you lying in the street, but my good nature wouldn't allow it."

"Still ain't no reason to leave a man in a stall all night. I woke up wonderin' if you'd rode on."

"Well, I didn't. You want to spend the morning grousing, or get some breakfast?"

"I could sure enough stand something to eat long as you're buyin'. You are buyin', ain't you?"

"I'll stand you a quick meal over at the café," Cole said, and flipped a silver dollar that Digger snatched out of the air.

"We're leaving in ten minutes. Meet me down at the constable's office. I need to pay a visit."

"What for?"

"Just professional courtesy."

Bone Blue and Little Boy, Bone's Negro assistant, were playing whist when Cole walked in. He knew both men from his days as a deputy

"Bone," he said as he took off his hat and knocked the dust from it against his leg.

"Holy Jesus!" Bone said. "Heard you was fertilizer in some widow's vegetable garden in Kansas."

"Everybody I run into lately has me killed in a different place," Cole said.

They shook hands, and then Cole shook hands with Little Boy, who wasn't right in the head from a horse kick a long time back. Little Boy grinned and rolled his eyes.

"Judge Parker send you to help out Jimmy Wild Bird?" Bone asked. He looked like he'd put on weight since last Cole had seen him. His belly hung over his belt like a haunch of pork.

Cole told him Parker had asked him to come.

"You'd be about the last man I'd expect. How many he send with you?"

"Just me. I hired a bounty man to assist."

Bone shook his head.

"Judge Parker lay it out for you, the troubles we've got over here?"

Cole assured him Parker had.

Bone shook his head again and slapped an ace on the table. "Well, I'm sure Jimmy's going to dance a jig about all the help he's getting from Fort Smith. Damned if he won't have to." Bone played the last of his hand and said to Little Boy: "You now owe me thirty-three-thousand dollars and several horses and most of the land from here to Nebraska." Little Boy grinned and rolled his eyes some more and said, yes, he supposed he did.

"Come on, I'll ride out with you to Jimmy's," Bone said, putting on his black felt hat.

"Suit yourself."

Joe Digger was just crossing the street from the café, grease glistening in his beard, when Cole walked out with Bone. Digger picked his teeth as he walked.

"That your posse man?" Bone wondered. Cole said it was, and Bone said: "You know, if I remember right, he threatened to kill Jimmy once over a prisoner."

"That so?"

"Judge might just as well have sent Cherokee Bill as you two the way Jimmy's going to act once he gets a load of you."

Cherokee Bill was a wild hair that had been terrorizing the territory on and off for a time and no friend of the law. They waited for Digger, then walked down and got their horses, and rode north.

"Jimmy lives up near Sugar Creek," Bone explained. "About an hour from here at a good lope."

When they rode into view of the cabin, Cole saw her standing on the porch, a broom in her hands, and his heart quickened. Then she looked up and their eyes met and Cole's heart quickened more.

Jimmy stood in the yard, his hands resting on the butts of his revolvers and his gaze steadfast on them as they rode up. Cole wondered in that brief instant if Anna had ever told Jimmy about them. Then they drew rein and Jimmy's gaze shifted from Cole to Joe Digger, then to Bone.

"Why you bringing these men here?" Jimmy said.

Anna hadn't moved.

Bone ran a finger over the brim of his hat and said: "They're the help the old boy sent you from Fort Smith."

"I asked for deputies."

"You want to say your mind," Cole said, "go on and say it, but say it to me directly."

His dark eyes flashed with anger. "Get off my land."

"Suits me to hell and gone," Joe Digger said. "I'll just round up that white sum-bitch, Caddo Pierce, and be on my way."

"Hold up," Cole said.

Bone rode his horse a step closer to Jimmy, leaned, and said: "Don't be a fool. Nobody said you all had to go to kissing and sleeping in the same bed. I thought you wanted them killers caught."

"The only thing will get caught is me getting a bullet caught in my back," Jimmy said, his gaze now fully on Joe Digger.

"Nobody will shoot you in the back," Cole said.

"Come on in the house and let's talk, Jimmy," Bone said. "Just me and you."

The lawman's jaw unknotted and his eyes assented. Bone Blue dismounted, then the two men walked inside the house.

"You might have told me you and Jimmy Wild Bird had a history," Cole said.

"Wasn't much of one," Digger said. "He had a prisoner I wanted for the reward, wouldn't give him up, and we about went to gun play over it. Water under the damn' bridge far as I'm concerned."

"You mind watering our stock?" Cole asked Digger. He grunted, then took the horses to the water tank.

Cole looked at Anna. She hadn't moved. The only thing that had changed about her, if anything, was that she was even more breathtaking. Cole could feel his blood ticking in his wrists.

Then she said, as though they were all strangers who had stopped in their travels: "Are you men hungry?"

Joe Digger was too far away to hear her question, but Cole said: "If you have coffee, it would be appreciated."

She nodded, went inside the house, and came back out again with two tin cups, and handed one to Cole.

"Anna," Cole said.

"I thought at first it wasn't you, that it couldn't be you," she said, glancing over her shoulder toward the house before speaking his name. "John Henry, I thought. . . ."

"That I was dead, killed in a dozen places?"

"Yes."

"There's a lot I need to tell you."

She closed her eyes as if suffering some sudden pain she could not speak of. "No," she said, shaking her head. "Jimmy doesn't know about us. I never told him."

Cole looked at the house instinctively, then over to where Digger was watering the horses. "We need to talk."

"Not now."

"I have to talk to you, Anna." It was all Cole could do to

60

keep from taking her in his arms.

She averted her eyes, then Digger came over and thanked her for the coffee, and blew on it before sipping it. His gaze traveled over her and she saw the way he was looking and turned and went back inside the house.

"Good coffee," he said, and that was his only comment. He drifted back over to where the horses were and took a bottle of whiskey from his pack and found himself a tree stump to sit on and commenced to lace his coffee and take it that way.

Soon Jimmy and Bone came out of the house and walked to where Cole stood, loosening the cinch on the General.

Jimmy spoke first. "I'd like to leave first thing in the morning. I've got to ride to town and get supplied."

"That will be fine," Cole said.

Jimmy looked to where Joe Digger sat, drinking his whiskey coffee. "We had a row one time, over a prisoner."

"So I've just learned. Don't concern yourself. He's only after one thing."

"What's that?"

"Reward money on the white man."

"That man will be my prisoner when we catch them."

"No," Cole said. "You can have the others, but the white man will be Digger's to take back to New Mexico for reward money."

Jimmy's eyes narrowed.

"That's the deal, take it or leave it," Cole said.

"What about you?"

"What about me?"

"You want something, too?"

"No," Cole said, "I don't want anything. I'm just doing an old friend a favor." Cole could see that Jimmy knew it was a lie, but he didn't challenge it.

"Bone vouches for you," he said. "That's good enough for me."

Cole looked at Bone who shifted his weight and looked away. "Then we'll leave first light," Cole said.

Later, Cole watched as Bone and the policeman rode off toward Talaquah. It hadn't escaped Cole's attention that Jimmy did not kiss Anna good bye. He busied himself with unpacking his animals and turning them out into the greasewood corral. Digger found a slab of shade on the backside of the house and lay down in it, his bottle propped in the crook of his arm.

"*Siesta*," he said, then tugged his hat down over his eyes.

Cole went into the house and found Anna sitting at the kitchen table, a cup of coffee in front of her. The light was dim, the cabin cool, and she looked up at Cole when he entered.

"Why?" she said.

"Why what?"

"Why did you leave without telling me?"

"I'll tell you now."

She shook her head. "Now's too late."

"No, let me tell you."

She looked away, and Cole walked over behind where she sat and placed his hands on her shoulders and said: "I'll tell you now."

She didn't turn around or look at him.

Cole spoke her name and told her nothing had changed for him. "All that time that's come and gone," he said, "nothing ever changed. I thought maybe it would, but seeing you, I know that it hasn't."

She stood up and turned toward him, and he could see the small lights trapped in the obsidian eyes, like pinpoints of silver.

"My heart called to you in the silence," she said. "For endless days, my heart called to you. And I watched for you on the road, thinking you would hear and come back to me. But you never did, and after a long time, my heart fell silent."

"Don't," Cole said. His hands found her hair and it felt like threads of silk, and she shook her head as if to tell him no. "I can't help it I feel the same."

"You have to," she said. "I'm married."

"That doesn't change my heart."

"John Henry. . . ."

That's when he kissed her.

CHAPTER SEVEN

He had no gun, no horse, and no money to buy either. But on that morning when he decided to burn the cabin, he swore a blood oath against the men who killed the woman. They would have laughed at him. An old man who didn't even have a horse to ride and no gun to shoot with—they would have laughed. But he wasn't so old that he had forgotten the way he used to be before he met the woman and had fallen in love with her. It was because of her he'd changed, had given up the old ways, and left Mexico and Texas behind him. Now he had no reason to stay the way he'd promised her. His heart was full of darkness that was darker than spilled blood.

He walked for two days and then a wagon came by on the third.

"Where are you going, old man?" the driver said. The driver was a black man, elderly, a head full of white hair like Texas cotton. He wore no hat and had some hair growing on his chin as well. And when the man spoke, one gold tooth caught the sunlight.

"I'm going that way," Pablo said, pointing straight ahead.

The black man looked off down the road. "What's that way?"

Pablo shrugged and said: "I don't know."

The black man said: "You can come up here and ride with me for a while if you want. I'm going that way, too."

It took a great deal of effort for him to climb up on the wagon, for he had only eaten some raw *nopales* from which he had scraped the thorns over the last several days. They had made his bowels loose, and this, along with the long walk and his suffering, had left him weak.

"Where you comin' from, you don't mind my askin'?" the black man said as he snapped the reins over the rumps of his mules.

"Back there," Pablo said without giving more than a slight nod of his head as to where back there was.

The black man swiveled his head around, looked, saw nothing, didn't remember anything back the way the old man was indicating except a trace running off the main road he'd seen a day or two ago.

"Back there?" he said. "Man, I ain't seen nothin' since I come up across the border. This is mighty lonesome country."

Pablo said nothing. His head drooped, his chin touching the top button of his shirt.

The black man was still talking when he realized the old Mexican was asleep, sitting upright.

Pablo dreamed of the woman, dreamed of shadows crossing the darkness, dreamed of fire.

Late that afternoon the wagon came to a halt and Pablo came instantly awake.

"Be stoppin' for the evenin', mister," the black man said as he climbed down off the wagon seat and began unhitching his team. "Good grass here and a little water." A small stream cut through the tall grass. There were blackjack trees of gnarly wood you couldn't sink an axe into and the soil was red dust.

Wordlessly Pablo climbed down from the wagon and began lending a hand with the mules.

"Name's George," the black man said across the rump of one of the mules. "George Pepper. Some calls me Black George. I'm a trader."

Pablo led the off-hand mule over to the water to drink. The

black man followed along with the other mule.

"What do you trade?" Pablo asked as they allowed the mules to drink.

"Trade anything," he said. "Got me a whole wagon full of tradin' things. Watches, shoes, traps, fry pans, egg beaters, ladies' corsets, bitters, cigars . . . you name it, I trade for it."

Pablo looked around at the wagon.

"What I don't trade, I sell," George said. "Maybe I could sell you something."

Pablo looked at him. "No. I have no money."

"Well, maybe we could trade for somethin', then."

"You got any pistols?"

"Got one or two, I reckon. I'd have to dig around in my wagon to find 'em."

Pablo nodded.

"First, we'll have us a little supper," George said. "Don't like conductin' business on an empty stomach. Marfa says it's bad luck."

"Who's Marfa?"

"A nice woman I once knew, in Iowa," George said. "Don't suppose you ever been to Iowa."

"No. This is as far as I got."

George fried salted ham in an iron skillet. Its sweet spicy smell drifted out of the pan and mixed with the pungent wood smoke and that of coffee brewing in a tin pot. Pablo thought he might faint from the hunger the smells stirred in his belly.

George sliced some bread and laid it in the pan grease to fry. Afterward he made sandwiches out of the affair.

The first few bites were difficult for Pablo; his stomach clenched at the first food it had known in several days. But he slowly chewed it and swallowed it in tiny bites until he grew accustomed to eating again.

George sat across the fire from him and devoured one

sandwich, then another, the meat grease dripping down his fingers.

When Pablo finished his first sandwich and began sipping some of the coffee, George said: "Have another, you look like you ain't et in a week."

Pablo gratefully accepted the offer. "My name is Pablo Juárez," he said.

"Well, nice to make your acquaintance, Mister Juárez." George offered him a greasy handshake. "Pardon the mess."

Pablo ate the second sandwich, taking his time, feeling guilty as he ate. The remembrance of his wife was sodden in his heart.

"Learned to cook when I was a cowboy down around San Antone," George said. "Hung out with some *vaqueros*. They taught me to rope good and cook and introduced me to their *señoritas.*" George sighed and stirred the embers and the orange light glowed against his black skin. "Ain't no better ropers than a *vaquero* and no better-lookin' gals than Mexican gals."

Pablo thought of Mexican girls and the woman and how none of the Mexican girls he had known compared to the woman. Then he shut the thoughts out of his mind. He told himself he'd have to remember her the way she was before the renegades came if he was to remember her at all without the gnawing feeling.

"Seen how you was sleepin' sittin' up, there in the wagon," George said. "Knowed right off you must've been a *vaquero* at one time or the other. A *vaquero* learns how to sleep sittin' up in his saddle, ridin' night hawk."

"Yes. I know," Pablo said.

George grinned. "Men like us," he said. "Ain't hardly none left this side of the Canadian. Things changed a lot. All the great trails nothin' but places in a man's mind now. White man has strung the whole countryside with barbed wire. Barbed wire and railroads. They about have ruined this country."

Pablo remembered the days of his youth, the days of horses and lariats floating through the dusty air, the sharp horns of wild cattle. The way a river smelled before you got to it.

"I always cussed them mossy horns and the dust I had to swallow all up and down them trails," George was saying. "The Chisholm, the Goodnight-Lovin', the old Western. Rode up them all. Cussed them all, too. All those long days and poor food and wild rivers. I don't cuss it no more, though. Truth is, I miss it."

"There is a lot to miss about the old days," Pablo said.

George smiled. "Let's get to tradin'."

It was amazing to Pablo how many items George Pepper had in the back of his wagon, everything imaginable, including an old McClellan saddle hanging from a rope, the leather nearly gone from the tree. George dug around through boxes of tools and kitchen utensils and pie plates and finally found the pistols.

"Well, that's them," he said, handing them to Pablo.

Pablo examined them. One was a Dragoon Colt, the other a Walker, each weighing nearly four pounds. The Dragoon had a pitted barrel and split wooden grips and he could see the firing pin was sheered off. The Walker seemed to be in good working order. Pablo thumbed back the hammer, pulled the trigger. The hammer fell with a sharp snap.

"It could maybe use some oilin'," George said. "But it shoots."

Pablo turned it over and over in his hands, tested the weight and heft of it. Everything brought a different memory.

"It's been converted over from black powder," George said. "Shoots regular cartridges. Belonged to a Texas Ranger."

Pablo handed it back to him.

"Don't suit you?" George said.

"As I said, I have no money."

"Well, you got anything you could trade?"

There was only the silver cross, the one he wore around his

neck, the one María had given him those many years ago. He removed it.

"This is all I have."

George took it and examined it. "Pure silver?" he asked.

"Yes."

George hefted it in his hand, turned it over. It wasn't much of a cross, no longer than his little finger. Still, what did he need with those old pistols?

"Deal," George said. "You take your pick of either of them pistols."

Pablo thought about it for a moment. The cross was the last connection with the woman, except for his memory of her. He could not get revenge with a small cross of silver. "OK," he said, and stuck the pistol in his belt.

"Naw, that won't do," George said, seeing how the pistol leaned so heavily out over Pablo's belt. "Let me take another look in the wagon."

He dug around some more, came out with an old holster and cartridge belt. The leather was cracked and brown and stiff. "Here," he said.

Pablo took it, buckled it around his waist, stuck the Colt in the holster. Three inches of the barrel poked through the end.

"Now you are a *pistolero*, Mister Juárez."

"No, not yet," Pablo said. "Not until I get some bullets to shoot."

George flashed a wide grin. "I'd trade you some bullets for that fine-lookin' pistol and belt," he said, " 'cept I ain't got no bullets to trade you wit'."

"First the gun, then the bullets, then a fine horse to ride," Pablo said. "Then I will be a *pistolero.*"

George said: "Yes, sir, I believe you will." Then he turned around and shook a little and said: "Night's gettin' chill. You a drinkin' man, Mister Juárez?"

CHAPTER EIGHT

The boy rode last in line behind the others. The memory of the old man was branded into his heart. He could still see the woman's dead eyes behind his own as the sun set, red beyond the tan hills. She had looked frightened, true enough, but had not cried out as the others set upon her. She spoke in a language he did not understand when they first set upon her. She'd come out of the cabin and saw Billy strike the old man with his pistol there in the shadow of the lean-to. She'd tried to go to him, but Caddo had grabbed her and said—"Not so fast, sister."—and the others had turned and looked at her in the same way they had looked at the Osage lawman's woman. Then he saw the death in her eyes.

He'd felt his spirit break, had felt the woman's blood washing over him like warm rain, and had heard the voice of his grandfather speaking to him as a crow, its wings glossy under the sun. Then his grandfather had flown across the sun just before it burst into brilliant red light. The crow's caw had echoed in his ears as the men had taken the woman back inside the house.

He had run to the corral in time to see the crow grandfather disappear beyond the hills, still crying, it had seemed, for the woman who would not. Then the sky had grown black as a storm.

When he'd gone back into the house, the woman was dead and the others were sitting around the table eating the meal she'd fixed them as though nothing at all had happened. Billy had asked him why he had not taken part in the game they'd played with her. He did not answer, then Billy called him something akin to a woman himself and laughed at him. The white man had been drunk and the others were getting that way on the liquor of the old man's they'd found. And the woman had lain still, there on the floor at their feet, a thing discarded.

Someone had said that they should kill the old man, too, but Billy had said they should leave him to die a slow death and why waste the bullets—because Billy hated everyone and the others went along with it. He had thought maybe he should slip away during the night once they were asleep and slit the old man's throat and do him a favor so that he would not have to die so slowly or see his wife's dead eyes. But when the others had finally slept, the only thing he could do was go to the old man to see if he had already died. And when he saw that he hadn't, he had lifted a canteen to the old man's lips and then crept away.

After they had ridden away, he had pretended to be angry and had said that he wanted to go back and cut the old man's throat and cut out his heart to prove that he was one of them and Billy, who had questioned his loyalty from the beginning, told him to go ahead and to bring the old man's heart back as proof.

He had hoped that when he arrived the old man *would* be dead, but he wasn't and so he'd gone and killed one of the pigs the old man kept and cut out its heart. Then he had undone the wire they'd tied up the old man with, before riding away with the heart in his pocket.

They had laughed when he'd arrived with the bloody thing, and Billy had looked at it and told him that to be a brave warrior, he must eat the heart, and so he had to prove he was not lying to them and that he was as brave as any of them. But mostly he had eaten the heart to choke down his secret.

That night he had had a vision that the crow had turned white and the sun had become a bloody eye that the white crow held in its beak, plucked from the face of the Great Maker. He had not known what the vision meant, but he had crept away from the camp and gagged the chunks of the heart from his guts and had fallen to his knees, tasting naught but his own bile.

Then the crow had come and perched on a branch of a cottonwood and told him this: *A man will come for you and he will be Death. And when he releases your spirit, you will forever wander in the great emptiness of a dry land without water or food or rest, and this will be your punishment.*

Then the crow had flown down from its perch and had taken one of the chunks of expunged heart in its beak and had flown away in a great flurry of wings. To the boy, it had been as though the crow had taken away his own heart and had left his sin in the remaining bloody fragments and for a long time it was hard for him to breathe. And when the vision or the reality had ended, he had felt death creeping into his blood—a vague black thing, blacker than the crow's feathered body.

CHAPTER NINE

On the other side of the wall they could hear the guttural gasps of Joe Digger as he slept, narcotized from the whiskey and the warm air. Anna's hands sought Cole's face there in the dim cool light of the cabin.

"How long will Jimmy be gone?" Cole asked.

"Usually when he goes to Talaquah, he is gone the day, but this time he may not be."

"It's easily an hour of riding each way."

She kissed Cole and Cole kissed her. He could feel the heat through her clothes, and old aches stirred in him in ways he couldn't describe. She led him to the bed behind a curtain.

"I should tell you to leave," she said.

"Is that what you really want?"

Her dusky skin felt fevered to Cole's touch. She kissed his wrists and the knuckles of his hand while he kissed her hair, felt the silken threads of it against his lips. He took in the scent of her and it was comforting and familiar. He wanted her more than he had any woman. She set his heart tripping over itself and the heat in him rose like a fever. But he knew they couldn't do this thing. As much as he desired her and she desired him, he couldn't take advantage of the situation and still ride out with her husband. If he allowed what was happening to go on, he'd have to leave the Settlements the same way he had the last time—feeling shamed for his failures.

"Anna," he said, and pulled away.

She looked at him, her dark eyes full of uncertainty, questions.

"I thought this was what you wanted," she said.

"I do, but not like this. I don't think it's really what you want, either. Tell me I'm wrong."

She folded her arms across her chest as if she were suddenly cold and turned away from him. She walked to the window and looked out at the metallic light.

"You're right," she said. "I don't even know what I think any more, John Henry. The world, my world, is a confused place for me."

He went to her, put his hands on her shoulders, but she wouldn't turn around and look at him.

"You are like the coyote," she said, "who shows his face when it is least expected, and then is gone again in a whisper. I thought I was over you, that you were just a memory, like an old photograph that I would sometimes look at but not be roused to anger or pity or hatred . . . or even love."

Cole kissed her hair and told her that he was sorry for all the pain he'd caused her, that his youth was his only excuse for being so foolish those many years ago in not returning at least to tell her that he was leaving Indian Territory.

"It doesn't matter now why you left then," she said.

Cole felt her shiver. "It does to me."

"I would have gone with you had you come for me," she said.

"I know."

"Then why didn't you come if you knew that?"

"Because it wasn't my right to take you away from your people, this land. I wasn't part of this place, and I knew your father would never allow it. I couldn't bring that disgrace on you."

"Men are such fools," she said. "They always think that they know what women want, and they never do."

"Are you speaking about me, or Jimmy?"

She turned quickly, fire in her eyes, and said: "Both of you, all of you!"

"Do you love him, Anna?"

"I don't know. He has become so distant from me. This thing, this craziness that is in him . . . I don't understand it. It has been like living with a stranger for the past year."

"Never any children?"

She blinked. "No," she said after a long moment in which Cole thought that she was going to cry, but, instead, she went to the stove and kindled a fire under the coffee pot.

"I'm sorry to hear it."

Without turning, she said: "Why? Why should you be sorry for my marriage? Why should you be sorry that I have no children?"

"I just am, Anna. I think of how it could have been between us, how. . . ."

"Please, let's not talk about it any more." Her voice was edged with anger.

The window fractured the sunlight and broke it into squares that lay on the puncheon floor and they were like two shadows, Anna and Cole, afraid to go to the light and be seen in it for fear of what they might show each other.

"Why did you really come back?" she asked.

"To see you again."

"What about him? Will you help him?"

"Yes. I'll help him." Something broke in her. Cole could hear the half utterance of her emotions. He rolled a shuck and smoked it, leaning against the doorjamb and stared out into the empty places of the land, toward the sky where a crow flew alone, winging its way across the sea of endless blue. "It took me a long time to stop thinking about you every day," he said.

"We break each other's hearts and wonder why," she said.

"I had nothing to offer you then, and, even if you weren't married, I'd have nothing to offer you now."

She took a pair of cups down from the cupboard and set them on the rough table, then took the pot and filled them with steaming coffee.

"You think that's what women want? A man who can offer them something."

"Don't they?"

She shook her head and sat before one of the cups and took it into her hands, blowing steam from the surface before nibbling at it.

"They want only one thing," she said.

"A man who will love them."

"Yes, a man who will love them and never leave them."

Cole sat down opposite her. "You want to ride away with me now?"

"I'm not sure, John Henry. Honest to God." She looked at him from across the space of the table, but he could see it in her eyes that were he to say then and there that he wanted her to come with him, that they'd ride away and never look back, the answer would have been no.

They heard Joe Digger grunting and stirring outside the cabin and looked into the mirror of their coffee cups. Cole reached across the table and touched her hand with his. "I really am sorry for everything," he said.

"Me, too." She sipped her coffee and stared into his face. "I still love him in spite of everything. And I still don't want him to die out there. So I'm asking you to. . . ."

"I'll do what I can," Cole said. "But the truth is, none of us may come back from this. You have to prepare yourself for the worst, Anna."

She flinched. "I want him to come back . . . and I want you to come back."

"That's a lot of wanting."

"I know it."

"And if we do both come back? Then what?"

They heard the horses nicker in the corral.

"That's probably Jimmy returning," she said.

Cole stepped outside, saw Joe Digger leaning over the back of his horse, watching him.

"You enjoyin' yourself?" he said.

He looked at cabin, then back down the road where Jimmy was riding into view.

"Looks like the constable's coming back. I suspect an Indian can be a mighty cantankerous son-of-a-bitch if he thinks his woman has got eyes for another man, wouldn't you?"

"Mind your own business."

"Sure, sure. It ain't none of my concern what people do. But let me tell you this, John Henry. I ain't rid all this way just for the Sunday pleasure of it. I came here to kill some men and take that white sum-bitch back to New Mexico for the reward. That still your aim, or has it changed in the last couple of hours?"

Cole walked over to where Digger stood. Jimmy Wild Bird was a couple of hundred yards from reaching the house.

"Nothing's changed for me," Cole said. "Keep your thoughts to yourself. And one more thing. We get on the heels of those renegades, you leave off with the drinking. You understand?"

His gaze narrowed. "I guess we each got us a temptation we oughten to have. I'll keep off the liquor and you keep your mind on the business at hand. Maybe that way, we'll both come out of this alive."

Cole was tempted to send him packing, but he could see no way of doing it without a fight.

Jimmy Wild Bird rode up to the house. He had several sacks of supplies tied to his saddle horn. He dismounted, looked in the direction of the two men, and then went into the house without a word.

"Man comes home, probably hungry and wantin' his supper," Digger said, turning his attention to the currycomb in his hand. "Maybe wantin' something more than just his supper."

Cole turned and walked toward the water tank, dipped his bandanna in it, and tied it around his neck, cool and wet. His mind was feverish with anger and shame. Then he rolled himself a shuck, and smoked it. When he finished, he took the Winchester and walked off toward the copse of trees several hundred yards from the house. He thought he'd heard a wild turkey gobble. But mostly he just wanted to be alone, away from the cabin and the thought that Jimmy was inside with Anna. Or maybe it was just knowing that what he had wanted to do with Anna had been wrong, and he didn't want to look into the man's eyes whilst they sat at the supper table.

Cole stayed in the woods until the sun filtered low through the trees and threw long shadows. He heard Jimmy call from the house that supper was on but still he stayed in the woods until the sky turned a deep velvet, before he went back.

There were lights on inside the cabin. When Cole walked in, Anna and Jimmy and Joe Digger were sitting around the table, their plates scraped clean—except for Anna's, which was barely touched. Jimmy looked up and said: "What happened . . . you get lost out in them woods?"

Cole told him he thought he was onto a turkey but never got a shot at it. Jimmy said there were some wild turkeys around sometimes, but he hadn't been able to shoot one, either. Joe Digger poured whiskey into his tin cup, drank at it, and watched Cole with his hooded, brooding eyes.

Cole ate little, and Jimmy said they could sleep on the porch if they wanted, for it looked like it might rain and the roof over the porch was well repaired and wouldn't leak and get them wet. Anna avoided Cole's glance as he carried his plate to the basin where she stood, drawing water into the sink from a pump.

Cole lay on the porch for a long time after they'd tossed down their sougans and watched the lightning off in the distance and heard the soft rumble of thunder. His thoughts were of earlier in the day. None of it made him feel good about himself, and for the first time in a long while he felt like he'd crossed lines and broken codes a man wasn't allowed to do, at least not a good man.

Joe Digger mumbled in his sleep, mumbled the same names he had before when he was drunk—that of a woman and a child—and spoke of graves and saving the boy. From somewhere out in the woods an owl hooted spookily.

The coming storm, a bird of prey, a drunken killer's nightmares, Anna inside with her husband. All of it put a coldness in Cole and reminded him that everyone was forever tied to his past, to the darkness and wandering ghosts and wounded spirits of his life. He felt the full weight of his own mortality bearing down on him so hard he could scarcely breathe. His own sleep didn't come until long after the yellow light within the house went out.

CHAPTER TEN

They passed a farmhouse with some pretty good-looking horses. Pablo noticed the horses and thought to himself that maybe such a horse was exactly what he needed. He waited until they had gone for another mile or two—he couldn't be sure exactly—but he calculated it to be far enough.

"You can let me off here," he said.

"Here?" George said, looking around.

"Yes, my friend," Pablo said. "This will be far enough for me."

George hauled back on the reins and the mules' ears pricked up and they stood shuddering in their traces. "You for certain, Mister Juárez?"

"Yes," Pablo said.

"Well, OK. I guess you know better'n me where it is you want to get off at."

"*Sí.*"

George hunched his shoulders and set the brake and watched as the old man climbed down. "Good luck to you, Mister Juárez."

"*Gracias, señor,*" Pablo said.

"Maybe we'll meet up again," George said. "I'll be around these parts tradin' until I decide to go somewheres else. I get so's after a while I like to see new places."

"Perhaps, *amigo.* Who is to say what the future holds?"

"That's right," George said with a grin. He offered Pablo his hand, and the old man shook it with a firm grip.

Pablo waited until the black man disappeared down the road, before turning and heading back toward the farm. It would be a bold trick and one that could easily get him shot if he were to fail at it. But he needed a horse.

It took the better part of an hour to get there because of the old ache in his right hip and because he still hadn't fully regained all of his strength. Sweat trickled down his neck and over his ribs and soaked his shirt.

The farm sat back off the road, down a lane where wagon tracks had scored the grass. He walked down that way toward the house. There were three other buildings besides the house—a chicken coop, a corncrib, and a tool shed. But what interested him most was the corral where the horses were standing, watching him, their ears up, their noses snuffling the air. One in particular caught his eye, a nice tall claybank with black stockings.

He walked up to the house, pretending not to notice the horses. There seemed no one about, but he must make sure. He removed his sombrero; the straw in the crown was frayed, and a new tear was beginning. He should have bought a new one when he and María had gone to town last, but he had been happy with the old one. He pulled the pistol and hid it behind the hat.

He knocked on the door and waited, standing, holding his hat and the pistol in his hands. In a few moments he heard footsteps from inside and then the door opened.

A man with a napkin hanging from the front of his shirt stood there, looking at him.

"Yes, what do you want?" the man asked.

"I am sorry, *señor,* to have to trouble you, especially at the hour of your dinner. But I could use a drink of water."

The man looked at him, then looked beyond him to see if

there was someone else with him. Then he looked back at him. He was a large man with a full head of hair the color of rust. He had a meaty face and a thick neck and round heavy shoulders.

"You lost?" the man asked. "I don't know of any Mexicans around this part of the country. You must be lost."

"Yes, maybe a little, *señor.*"

"Well, I reckon you can go on over and pump yourself up some water. But you git on down the road soon's you've finished getting a drink. You understand me?"

"*Si, señor.* I understand."

The man stood there, waiting for him to retreat.

Well, now what? It had been a long time since he'd done this sort of thing. He had to give it a little thought to see exactly how he should do it. He did not want to kill anybody just to get a horse. Then he remembered that he had no bullets for the gun. The man did not look like he would just give him one of his horses if he asked. Something had to happen. He was thinking that maybe he should just pull the pistol out from behind the hat and take his chances that the man would not notice that there were no bullets in it. Then, just as he was thinking about it, he heard a woman's voice from inside.

"Edwin, who is at the door?"

The man turned partway to look back into the room. "Just some old damn' Mexican begging a little water," the man said.

Well, when he turned back around, Pablo had the big Dragoon pistol aimed at his face. The man spoke half a word.

"Wha- . . . ?"

"Please, *señor,*" Pablo said, holding a finger to his lips. "Not so loud your wife will hear and come see you like this."

The man swallowed hard and when he did, the napkin he was wearing in the front of his shirt bobbed up and down.

"I only need a horse, and a saddle. Not too much to ask in

exchange for your life, eh?"

The man shook his head.

"Good," Pablo said. "Tell her you are going to be outside for a little while and that when you are finished, you will come back in and finish your dinner. Tell her that everything is all right."

The man swallowed again and the napkin moved again.

"Elsa, I'm going outside for a few minutes to take care of something."

"Well, don't be long, your dinner'll get cold."

The man stepped outside.

"I am going to put my pistol back under my hat in case your woman looks out. But I can get it back out again quick if I have to," Pablo said. "You believe that I can do it?"

"Yes," the man said.

"Good. Then let's go pick out a horse."

It was the claybank mare that had caught his eye earlier that he told the man he wanted. She had good conformation, and keen eyes and long legs. He liked his horses tall. She looked like she could run pretty fast.

"I will need a saddle, too."

The man said: "They're inside the shed. Take whichever one you want."

They stepped inside the shed and Pablo said: "That one will do."

The man said: "That's my best saddle."

"That is why I picked it," Pablo said. "Would you please put it on that pretty mare for me."

The man grunted as he picked up the saddle, more from disappointment, Pablo figured, than from the strain of lifting it.

"You sure must know horses," the man said as he saddled the claybank. "This one cost me five hundred dollars."

"Yes, I've always had a good eye for them," Pablo said.

The man finished saddling the horse and led her out the gate of the corral. "Anything else you'd like to steal from me while you're here?" he asked.

"Consider the horse a loan, *señor*. What is your name?"

"Edwin Black," the man said.

"Well, *Señor* Edwin Black, I will see that your horse is returned to you when I have finished my business."

He could see the look of mistrust in the man's eyes. *Well, believe what you like, señor, but I am a man of honor and will return your horse if I am still alive to do it,* he thought.

The man watched with growing dejection as Pablo climbed up in the saddle and took up the reins. Pablo made the mare side-step first this way, then that. It was a well-behaved horse.

"Now, one more thing I need from you, *señor.*"

"What?" Edwin Black said.

"Do you have a rifle?"

"Well, what if I said I didn't?"

"I would not believe you."

"No, I didn't think so."

"Call to your woman and tell her to bring it," Pablo said.

The man called toward the house and told the woman to bring his rifle. She appeared in the door.

"Is there something wrong?" she said, smoothing her palms against her waist.

The man seemed frustrated with her, then he said again that she should bring his rifle. She looked at Pablo, then at her husband. Then she turned and went back inside the house, and returned in a few moments, carrying the rifle. It was a heavy brass-fitted Winchester repeater.

The man started to take it from her, but Pablo said: "Here, let me see it."

"What's going on here, Edwin?" the woman said.

"Nothing, Elsa. Just that this man is stealing my best horse

84

and saddle and now my rifle, that's all."

"What?"

"Just be quiet, OK?"

"I will also need some bullets for it," Pablo said.

The woman looked at her husband.

"Go and get him a box of shells," the man said.

This time she didn't argue because of the way the man said it and looked at her as though he had no patience left for any more argument with her.

Pablo took some of the shells and loaded them into the rifle, and the rest he put in his coat pocket. Things were looking better now that he had a horse and a gun with bullets.

"Here," he said, taking out the old Walker. "You can have this. I doubt I would ever be able to find any bullets to fit it."

The man took the Walker and looked at it, then held it down along his leg knowing it was of no use to him.

"I will see that your horse gets returned to you as soon as I am finished with my business," Pablo said again. "And your saddle as well."

"What about the rifle?" the man asked.

"If I can," Pablo said. "That's yet to be seen." The man looked at his wife.

Pablo walked the horse back up the trace that led to the road, and, as he went, he could hear the woman talking to the man.

"Are you going to go after him and get back your horse and saddle and gun?"

"No," the man said. "I am going in to eat the rest of my dinner."

"Then you are just going to let him steal from us?"

"He's got the rifle, not me. Do you want me to get shot by my own rifle?"

"He's just an old man," she said.

"Maybe he is, but he looks like a man who's done this type of thing before. Did you see how he tricked me with this old pistol that didn't even have any bullets in it? That took some nerve. I could've shot him dead if I'd known. Son-of-a-bitch has some nerve!"

Pablo smiled at the words and touched heels to the mare and put her into a nice trot, memories of the old days racing through his mind, his blood afire.

★ ★ ★ ★ ★

BOOK II

★ ★ ★ ★ ★

CHAPTER ELEVEN

It was still raining when John Henry Cole shook loose of his bedroll the following morning and the smell of coffee coming from inside the cabin had a warming effect. But instead of going there, he went and saddled his horse, and helped Digger reload the pack animal.

"Gruesome day to set out after killers," Digger said.

Cole didn't reply. He worked efficiently, tying double knots and making sure the load was distributed evenly. They'd both been smart enough to carry slickers with them, but even wearing them, the rain spilled off the brims of their hats down their necks, and it didn't take long for their boots to end up soaked.

Cole heard the cabin door open and saw Jimmy Wild Bird come out, wearing a slicker as well and carrying a long gun. Anna stood in the doorway and Cole couldn't be sure, but he thought through the veil of rain that she tossed a glance in his direction. He had a hell of a feeling about everything, and he knew it was only going to get worse if he didn't get the chance to talk to her again before they left. But he couldn't see any way of that happening.

Jimmy Wild Bird came out to the corral and saddled his horse and packed the stocky little dun with supplies.

"There's hot coffee inside, you want," he said without making a formality out of it.

Digger said he had to visit the privy first. Cole took the opportunity to get a moment alone with Anna.

He poured himself a cup, and her presence in the room made it hard for him to get his words in line. "Have you thought more about what I said yesterday?" he asked.

"That's all I did last night was think about it."

"And?"

She shook her head. "I can't give you an answer. Not yet, anyway. I talked with Jimmy last night. I told him I was unhappy."

Cole sipped the scalding hot coffee.

"I'm not sure he understands," she said.

"He understands," Cole said.

"How can you be sure?"

"I saw the look in his eyes when he came out to the corral."

"He wouldn't talk to me about it," she said. "Now, there is no time."

They stood in the growing light, seeming to hold their breaths.

"I feel ashamed for what happened yesterday," she said.

"I do, too. But I have to tell you something."

"What?"

"If I had it to do over again, I'm not sure I wouldn't do the same thing."

"John Henry. . . ."

Cole saw Digger coming toward the house.

"I love you, Anna. You think about that while I'm gone."

She started to say something, and Cole could see it in her eyes that there was something tearing at her heart, but then they heard Digger's boots on the porch, and she turned her back to Cole, leaving whatever was on her mind unsaid.

Digger's silence as he drank his coffee was unnerving. He knew what Cole was thinking and Cole didn't like it. Cole didn't like anything about the situation. Something had begun that couldn't be finished, and he hated to leave unfinished business.

Then Jimmy came back to the cabin and the three of them

sat there, drinking coffee, and Anna served them hoecakes and blackstrap molasses and never sat down with them, choosing instead to keep herself busy at the stove, her back turned to them.

"You-all about ready to get on the trail?" Jimmy said, as they scraped their plates clean.

"Ready when you are, Officer," Joe Digger said. "I ain't gettin' any richer sittin' around here eating hoecakes."

The Indian looked at him. "Then let's get at it," he said, and they stood and placed their hats on their heads from where they'd rested them upside-down by their feet, and filed out the door, except for Jimmy, who said he'd catch up with them in a minute.

Cole and Digger sat their horses and waited for him. When he came out of the house, he wore a scowl and didn't say anything, but simply mounted up and rode out. They followed, Cole last in line. Cole tossed a look back over his shoulder and saw Anna standing in the doorway, watching them, the rain falling in a gray line, and then she stepped back into the shadows and was gone.

It had stopped raining by the time they rode into Shelby Flats—a sleepy little village that seemed to be big on weeds and stray dogs and not much else to recommend it. Jimmy Wild Bird said that the last killing had taken place right near there—an Osage policeman and his wife. Jimmy said a man was living there who could tell them more.

Faces appeared in doorways at their arrival, mostly Indians dressed in calico shirts and brogan shoes and carrying rifles.

"The man we have to see is named Ray Doolittle," Jimmy said. "He's about half Lipan Apache and half something else."

"Apache?" Joe Digger said. "I thought all the Apaches were over in New Mexico and Arizona."

"Ray ain't. He was a Light Horse once," Jimmy said. "Then he got shot in the knee and lost his leg."

"Where do we find Doolittle?" Cole asked.

"He has a place just over there," Jimmy said, pointing to a knoll a quarter mile beyond the village proper.

They walked their horses through the village with the dogs sniffing at the heels of their mounts. They saw a man squatting in the weeds, doing his business.

"Some place," Digger said, leaning to spit.

Ray Doolittle was in his yard when they rode up.

"I seen you coming," he said. "Up here, I can see 'most everything that goes on." He had a crutch propped under his arm, a high-back wheelchair sat nearby.

"Ray," Jimmy said. "We've come looking for those Creeks." Then Jimmy introduced the others.

Ray Doolittle leaned on the crutch and didn't bother to offer to shake hands. There was still some evidence of a strong, muscled body in his shoulders and arms, but he had a paunch over his belt and lacked the fine cheek bones of most Apaches. His face was as round as a fry pan. "Digger," he said. "I've heard of you."

Joe Digger said: "Well, I ain't surprised. I've caught many a fish outta this territory."

Then Ray turned his attention to Cole. "Heard of you, too. Deputy under Judge Parker, wasn't you?"

Cole didn't tell him he wasn't a federal man any longer or his real reason for being there now.

"What can you tell us about the killing?" Jimmy said.

"Step down and I'll tell you what I know," Ray said.

The day was turning sultry and the grasshoppers buzzed and popped out of the weeds as they dismounted. Ray Doolittle eased himself into the wheelchair and held the crutch across his lap.

"It was late," Doolittle began. "Sun was almost set when they came riding in. I seen them from that window over there. I was sick in bed that day. I get sick sometimes with the fever . . . it comes and goes ever since I got my leg taken off. Anyway, I watched them . . . five of them . . . riding slow, like they wasn't in no hurry, like they was just looking around at things, getting the lay of where everything was. The light was getting weak, but I could tell that one of them was a white man. You can always tell a white man by the way they'll ride a horse . . . different than an Indian. Them others was Indians. They just rode on through and I was glad they did. Glad until I seen where they were headed . . . out to Cecil Tall Horse's place."

"The policeman?" Jimmy said.

"Uhn-huh. He's an Osage, but a good Osage. Least he was. Quiet man, done his job. He was married to a Cherokee, real tall woman. Tallest woman most of us ever seen. Cecil and her were an item around here for a time when he first brought her here. But she was all right, did good by everybody. Got so nobody seemed to notice she was such a tall woman after a while."

It was lonely talk, Cole thought, the talk of a man too long without company.

"I watched them ride out there," Doolittle continued, pointing with his nose off to the west. "I thought to myself, what do those boys want with Cecil? If it wasn't for the fever, I'd've gotten out of bed and gone out there myself, 'cause it didn't feel right to me . . . them boys riding out to Cecil's so close to evening like that. Hitching up the buggy ain't no easy chore for me, but I'd've done it if it hadn't been for the fever that night. I watched and watched until it got too dark to see. Cecil lives just beyond that little rise . . . can you see it?" They turned and looked. "Anyway, I must've fallen off to sleep a time or two 'cause of the fever. But then sometime late, real late, I seen it, the fire. I knew it was Cecil's burning up. And I know it had something to do with them boys."

Ray Doolittle stopped and let out his breath through his nose; a look of utter despair crawled over his face. "Wasn't nothing I could do. I kept hoping somebody'd see it besides me, but nobody did. The next morning I crawled out of bed and hitched the buggy . . . took me two hours, but I did it . . . and went and got somebody. By the time we got out there, there wasn't nothing left. We found Cecil and Lou burned up. It was an awful thing to have to see."

"Which way did those boys go after the fire?" Cole asked.

"I looked around for their tracks," Doolittle said. "They rode west, due west . . . looked to me like they was heading straight into No Man's Land."

"Well, that makes sense," Jimmy said. "They'd have to know that even if someone was foolish enough to follow them, it wasn't likely they'd be followed into that country."

"Nobody that's got any sense would go after them boys in No Man's Land," Ray Doolittle said. "I've been there." Then his eyes lowered to the missing leg. "Left a leg there. . . ."

"What's between here and there?" Cole asked.

"Nothing, Deputy. Nothing but snakes, bad water, and out-laws."

"Then that means sooner or later, they'll be coming back into the Settlements," Jimmy said.

"How do you know?" Joe Digger wondered.

"They'll get bored sitting around, doing nothing. They'll want to make some more bad medicine. They won't follow Caddo Pierce for long if he doesn't keep them happy, keep them murdering and raping and stealing."

"Jimmy's right," Cole said. "Renegade Indian boys won't follow anybody long if they get bored. Especially they won't follow a white man."

"I wished to hell I could go with you," Ray Doolittle said.

"I wish you could, too, Ray," Jimmy said. "Thanks for the information."

They watered their horses and gave them a blow while Cole smoked a cigarette.

As if unwilling to have them leave, Ray Doolittle said: "You are welcome to stay for supper." It was just past noon.

"We have to go," Jimmy said.

"They burned Cecil and his wife up in their house," Ray said. "They probably did some terrible things to them before they burned them up. Lou was a handsome woman with all that long hair."

Jimmy nodded, then they mounted and turned their horses toward the west road.

"I feel sorry for him," Jimmy said as they rode away. "Just as soon be dead as to be crippled up like that."

"I'd put a bullet in my brain was I to lose a leg," Joe Digger said. "Man without his legs ain't much."

They rode in silence, the three of them, each a man with a different thought on his mind.

They camped that night near a river—Cole didn't know which one—and ate, remaining silent as they had been since leaving Doolittle's.

"You ever been into No Man's Land?" Jimmy finally said, looking across the campfire, the flames dancing in his eyes.

"I've been there a time or two," Cole said.

"Then you know we won't find anyone to help us up in that country."

"I know."

"Still some decent folks live there, but they won't say anything if those boys haven't molested them."

The fire crackled and it sounded like bones breaking. Joe Digger spat into the fire, spilled some whiskey in his cup, and offered it around. Jimmy Wild Bird declined but Cole accepted and took a pull, then handed it back with a warning look. Digger's hooded gaze told Cole he hadn't forgotten their agreement and he said: "Just a little something to keep the chill out."

Cole could see in the Indian's eyes that his mind was full of Anna, the way he stared into that fire as though trying to see the future dancing in the flames. He rolled himself a shuck and thought about Anna, too, and wondered what she had wanted to tell him. He smoked and watched the fire burn down and tried not to think so much about his sins, but it was hard not to do.

"Look at them stars fallin'," Joe Digger said.

Cole looked up and, sure enough, the stars were falling, one every few seconds. Jimmy looked up, too, then after a moment lowered his gaze back to the fire. "It's a bad thing when the stars fall," he said.

Joe Digger looked at him hard, the corner of his mouth twitching. "Leave off with that *Indian* talk," he said.

"You don't believe it?"

"No, I don't. I believe in this," Digger said, jerking his pistol. "I believe you put a bullet in a man, he stops breathin'. I believe you offer a whore enough money, she'll go with you. I believe sour mash is the best whiskey there is goin'. But I don't believe stars fallin' out of the sky mean a damn' thing!"

Even so you could tell Digger was uneasy with such talk and he slopped some more whiskey down his gullet as he looked back up at the falling stars. You could see it in his face. He wasn't any more sure of the unknown than the rest of them. Then the wings of something heavy fluttered through the darkness and embers popped in the fire. Then silence, utter and complete silence as in a tomb.

CHAPTER TWELVE

She had a dream the first night they were gone in which she saw them lying in black coffins with glass tops and that, below the glass, their faces were in serene repose. Jimmy lay in the middle with John Henry Cole to his right and Joe Digger to his left. Their hair was combed and their mustaches waxed, except for the bounty man's whose cheeks and neck were rough with stubble. A brass band played a funeral dirge and the mourners, instead of being dressed in black, were dressed in bright colors: reds and blues and yellows. And instead of it being a mournful time, there was great celebration—laughter and drinking and the men were chasing the women around and around, being lewd with one another, and she couldn't understand it and woke with a start, her heart hammering in her chest.

My God, she thought, and rose from the bed and went to the window and looked out, then went to the door and opened it and stepped onto the small porch to see if their horses were there in the corral.

Moonlight filled the yard in a pale swath and the corral stood empty except for the small palomino mare Jimmy had left her. The mare stood sleeping. The night air was cool and silver-black, and when she looked up, she saw the stars falling. She felt a hand on her back and turned, but no one was there. An owl hooted and a coyote answered and the world seemed to tilt, and she felt herself going off the edge into the abyss. She thought she heard a child cry and involuntarily she uttered the name: "Thomas . . . ?" Then she felt her world spin away and the dream returned time and time again that night, full of laughter and dead men and the cries of a child.

★ ★ ★ ★ ★

BOOK III

★ ★ ★ ★ ★

CHAPTER THIRTEEN

Her name was Hester Price and she'd once lived in Darke County, Ohio, and had been girlhood friends with Phoebe Ann Moses who was making a name for herself as a trick shot with Buffalo Bill's Wild West Show as Annie Oakley. But that was a long time ago and back then Phoebe Ann was just like every other girl except in one way—she was determined not to live and die in obscurity in Darke County, and she could shoot a rifle better than any man.

Hester had felt much the same about living and dying in obscurity. But a girl had few options in that rather somber country. She could content herself with marrying one of the local boys and thereby enter a life of raising crops and children, attending quilting bees and church socials, all the while trying and trying to survive child-bearing, cholera, diphtheria, and boredom. Or, a more ambitious and adventurous young woman could head into the wild West, where word had it that even a homely woman could do well for herself among the vast hordes of single, lonely, and desperate men who'd gone to seek their fortunes in the gold fields and silver mines. They'd carried with them dreams but no women.

For Hester, there was little decision to be made. She went West, just as Phoebe Ann was to do two years later. But unlike Phoebe Ann who'd married and gone respectable, Hester's opportunity to escape came in the guise of a scoundrel named Jack Hayworth—a whiskey peddler and part-time actor in whose handsome eyes her own dreams had begun to unfold. But the relationship lasted only as far as St. Louis, where Jack ran off with a platinum-haired actress.

Hester had just long enough to be properly broken-hearted before she met a man named Arkansas Ed who turned out to be a pimp and a gambler and not very good at either. But he was even handsomer than Jack Hayworth and a handsome man was her constant weakness. Somewhere amid the flurry of their romance, Arkansas Ed introduced her to the world of opium dens, and the vices of dope. But bad as it would sometimes get, she told herself it was still a lot more interesting than lonesome cicada-filled nights in Darke County, Ohio. Vastly better than muffled talk among the men about the weather and plowing and harvesting. And certainly more stimulating than standing with women in the kitchen, talking about the men.

Then Arkansas Ed got himself stabbed in a card game over a $5 pot in Tulsa and that's where she ended up working to survive—as a crib girl—the lowest form of prostitute, until Mr. St. John came along and made her a better offer. Mr. St. John was a hollow-eyed, slightly emaciated man, but dashingly handsome with his neatly trimmed mustaches and fine clothes. And he was as charming as ten devils. He had first seen her in the company of another man, a big Swede whose principal pleasure was to get mean drunk and abusive to her but whose generous supply of money did much to keep her from starving. Mr. St. John introduced himself, and when the Swede took offense, Mr. St. John showed him a two-shot Derringer that he wore in a snap rig just inside his coat sleeve at the wrist.

"This little gun will kill you twice," Mr. St. John had said to the Swede. "Trust me, it's done it before." The Swede took to his heels and Mr. St. John took her to dinner at the finest restaurant in Tulsa and introduced her to his companion, a younger woman named Lottie, to whom Mr. St. John referred often as "Pleasure". Then sometime during the course of the evening—which ended up with the three of them back at Mr. St. John's hotel room—he took to calling Hester "Delight".

"You are a sheer delight," he'd said. "And that's what I'll call you. Delight for you and Pleasure for Lottie. How would you ladies like to work for me?"

At first she'd laughed, just as Lottie had, just as they all had, but somewhere in the night, after so many bottles of champagne and several cocaine pills, she'd found herself in bed with them and it wasn't a complete surprise to her—for they had surpassed a point of sanity—and ended up falling asleep in one another's arms. And in the morning, Mr. St. John had taken them to breakfast and afterward bought them each two new dresses and asked them to join him in a new venture. Hester had inwardly denied herself because her experience with handsome, charming men thus far had proved her misfortune. Mr. St. John was a smoother talker than either Jack Hayworth or Arkansas Ed, and he'd rightfully argued what had she to lose except the dust of Tulsa and the stigma of being a crib girl? In return, he had said he would make each of them equal partners and that all monies from their endeavor would be split three ways.

She'd asked what sort of venture exactly was he talking about and he'd raised his eyebrows and smiled slyly and said: "There is only one business that men and women do here on the frontier that is worth a spit and a nickel. But I can assure you it is a good deal better than what you lovelies have been doing, and I won't abuse you and I will look out for you and not allow anyone else to abuse you." Then he'd explained to them that he had a little crossroads enterprise two days' ride out of Tulsa—a sort of saloon, general store, and whorehouse combined whose business was suffering since the loss of his last two girls.

"What happened to them?" Pleasure had asked. She was a strawberry blonde with a dime-size mole on her left cheek and large innocent eyes and her skin was nearly translucent and flawless. Her innocent manner and beauty made her easy to like.

"Why, one got married and the other saved her money and went off to college in Boston," Mr. St. John said. "It happens. I find myself about once a year in need of a new girl or two, and I knew the minute I laid eyes on you two, you were the ones. How about it?"

Well, what was she to do? She had little money, and though her dream had been someday to go to California, it may as well have been to go to China. Pleasure, *neé* Lottie Berg, had immediately accepted Mr. St. John's offer. "I have always been a sucker for a man with flattering lips and loose purse strings," she had said.

"It's still whoring, ain't it?" Hester had asked.

"It is, but tell me this, my sweet, what in this cruel and untamed world ain't?" Mr. St. John had replied.

So she'd thrown her few possessions in a carpetbag and climbed on the seat between Mr. St. John and Pleasure and the three of them rode to Greasy Junction and took up residence in the rear apartment of his establishment. It wasn't exactly California but it was a far cry from the cribs of Tulsa and boredom of Darke County.

Mr. St. John had stuck to his word and had divvied up the whoring money and had protected them from drunks and unruly buffalo hunters. He had also fed them well, always cooking the meals himself, and pampered them with kind words and gestures and washed their backs in his big zinc tub that he pulled out every Wednesday and Friday night and filled with hot water. He insisted they bathe at least twice weekly, more if they so chose.

Mr. St. John had also let it generally be known that barring holidays, Sunday was a day of rest for his girls unless, of course, some cowboy or drummer hadn't gotten the word and stopped in and couldn't be dissuaded to wait until Monday. On Sundays he drove them to the river where they had picnics and swam and played like children—Mr. St. John sometimes joining them in the water, but mostly content to watch them frolic while he sat on the bank, smoking his clay pipe and reading a small book he always kept in his possession.

Mr. St. John loved books and had a whole wall lined with shelves that held every manner of book on every subject imaginable. When Hester had asked him about the red book he carried, he'd replied: "It's a book of poetry by a fellow named Keats. They say he's pretty good, and when I learn to read, I'm going to read his book first." She offered to read it to him, but he proudly refused.

It all seemed rather odd and exotic in some ways, living with Mr. St. John and Pleasure. They were like a small family that the greater world had abandoned, a family that had to survive on its own without the benefit of kindness of others. And though men came and went in the constant pursuit of their earthly pleasures, and paid well for it, she felt unaffected by their passing. At times, when there were no patrons lingering about and it was simply the three of them, Mr. St. John would sit in his rocker before the fire with the red book open on his lap and his eyes would move over the words while Lottie brushed her hair, and she would find herself wishing him the ability to read the words aloud, knowing that words would bring comfort to them all. The feel of the brush coursing through her own hair, the crackle of embers, and the silence of the night outside their door seemed to her like a time of her childhood, a time of innocence returned. And sometimes she would think of Phoebe Ann Moses who shot glass balls out of the air, and wondered if she was equally happy and equally lost in that world of bareback riders, wild Indians, and stampeding buffalo, wondered if she and Annie's paths would ever cross and if they would talk about men and exotic roamings.

Mr. St. John would often pause in his supposed reading and look at them and say: "My, but aren't you both as lovely as lilies." And she knew that she had fallen in love with him, just as deeply as Pleasure had. Their love became like a circle. And for Hester, the circle would always protect them from the outer harshness that lay beyond the timbered walls and the crossroads that led down from Tulsa and out toward Talaquah and other unknown places. Then in the midst of her newfound happiness, the riders came.

CHAPTER FOURTEEN

Jimmy Wild Bird, John Henry Cole, and Joe Digger rode for four days into the west, each day riding until the sun stood low on the horizon and threw its blinding light into their eyes. On the fourth night, Joe Digger's pack horse got into some gypsum weed and ran off, and they had to trail it the next morning into a box cañon where they found it, or what remained of it. Someone had butchered the animal, taking the haunches, heart, and liver, and leaving the rest to the buzzards that flew off with great flapping wings as they approached.

"Damn and Jesus!" Digger exclaimed. "Somebody's done carved up my horse."

"Poor Indians," Jimmy Wild Bird said. "They found that horse and carved him up into meat."

"How do you know it was poor Indians?" Digger asked.

"Who else but a poor starving people would kill a horse for meat?" It seemed odd that Jimmy Wild Bird would talk about his own kind like that, but he seemed removed from the situation. "Let's go."

"I can't just let this here crime go unpunished," Digger said. "That was a damn' good pack horse up till now."

"What do you aim to do?" Jimmy said. "Go find them poor Indians and make them puke up your horse?"

Digger looked forlorn. Jimmy looked at the wheel of buzzards against the bright blue sky, the sun catching in their dark wings.

On the return to camp they came across a black man in a big

painted wagon hauled by a matching pair of mules. The mules were big jacks whose ears flicked and hides rippled along their ribs.

"How do, gentlemens," the black man said.

Digger looked at the man and spat.

"We're looking for five men," Jimmy said. "You seen any riders that add up to five?"

The black man shook his head. "Just seen one man, that was a few days ago, and he was walkin'."

"White man or Indian?" Cole inquired.

"Neither. He was a Spanish. *Vaquero.*"

"That ain't one of them, then," Digger said.

The black man looked at the wheel of buzzards and said: "Looks like something's died."

"Somebody killed and et my horse," Digger said. "It wasn't you, was it?"

The black man looked at him through tired, reddened eyes. "Why'd I want to eat a horse?"

"I don't know," Digger said. "I was just askin' if you did or not."

"No, sir. I ain't. I et a mule once, but that was because he keeled over on me when I was plowin' with him and I didn't get my corn planted and knew I'd have nothing to eat come winter. So, I et him instead."

"This Spanish," Jimmy Wild Bird said. "You say he was walking?"

"Yes, sir."

"Where was he walking to?"

The black man shrugged his shoulders, stared at the wheel of buzzards. More had joined in. "He didn't say. Said some men had killed his wife and he was goin' after them. He didn't even have a gun. I traded him one for this here silver cross." The man reached in the top of his shirt and showed them a silver cross threaded on a string of leather.

"Which way'd you run into the fellow?" Jimmy's lawman's brain was at work, calculating, putting things together. So was Cole's—it's a habit you learn if you wear a badge long enough. Little things come to big things, sometimes.

"Back yonder," the black man said, thumbing over his shoulder.

"No Man's Land," Jimmy said. "Sounds like those boys ain't through killing yet."

Digger leaned and spat and wiped his mouth, then said: "Well?"

Jimmy and Digger turned their horses in the direction the man had indicated. Cole rode up close to his wagon. "You armed?"

He said: "I got a sawed-off shotgun under the seat."

"Keep it handy."

"I always do."

"Best to stay alert."

He nodded, and Cole rode after the others.

Three days later they came to the burned-out cabin. "Looks like a grave over here," Jimmy said. "See how the ground's sunken in."

"Just one," Cole said.

"The Spanish's woman."

"Looks like."

"A man on foot," Digger said. "What chance in hell does he have?"

"I wouldn't count this one out," Jimmy said. "I know this old man. His name is Pablo Juárez and rumor has it he was a killer down along the Mexican border years ago."

"Shit," Digger said. "Old man afoot, I don't care if he was three killers down along the border."

Jimmy Wild Bird had a look in his eyes, a strange far-off look. "They'll murder lots more before we catch them," he said.

Digger rode around the camp in ever-increasing circles, leaning off the side of his saddle. Then he rode back to where Jimmy and Cole sat their horses.

"They ain't heading west no more," he said. "Tracks lead off that way." He pointed in a southeasterly direction.

"What's that way?" Cole said to Jimmy.

"Closest place is Greasy Junction."

"What's there?"

"Nothing much, just a whiskey den and whorehouse."

"If they get there before we do . . . ," Cole began, and didn't finish.

"Yeah," Jimmy said, nodding his head and tapping the ends of the reins in his palm. He was still looking off in the direction Digger had indicated. "Might be a way we can get there first."

"How's that, have our horses grow wings?" Digger asked. "They got at least a four, five day lead."

"You look at them tracks close?" Jimmy said.

"Sure I looked at 'em close."

"They look like they were riding hard?"

Digger shook his head.

"That's because they're in no hurry. They don't think anyone would be fool enough to follow them. They're taking their time, killing as they go. We ride cross-country, we might get there before they do. Be waiting on them."

Digger spat, said: "Well, hell's bells, what're we waitin' on?"

"We'll have to leave the pack animals to ride hard," Cole said.

"Leave them," Jimmy said, putting heels to his horse.

Digger looked at Cole. "I already left mine, back up in that box cañon. Remember?"

Cole had little choice but to ride after them but somewhere

in his head the thought formed that only fools rush in. Maybe that's what they were: fools.

CHAPTER FIFTEEN

Pablo Juárez had himself a fine horse and saddle and repeating rifle with plenty of bullets, but none of these could he eat, and game proved to be scarce with but a single sighting of some antelope far out of rifle range. It had been three days since he had robbed the man of his gun and horse.

"Maybe I should've stolen his dinner, also, eh?" he said to the horse as he rode along feeling the pains in his belly growing.

The horse tossed its head and stepped lively to the command of Pablo's knees and legs. The sky to the south was growing fat with gray and black clouds. A storm was building. Pablo could feel the storm gathering in his bones, the ache traveling the length of his back and into his hands.

"Maybe I should have stolen a blanket, too," he said.

Pretty soon he saw a house sitting not far off the road and rode over to it. When he came close enough, he saw the woman bent to work in a large garden where the corn stood taller than she, its green leaves shimmering in the sun; he could see, too, that she had some beans and squash planted.

He sat his horse for a long time and watched her, and if she saw him, she made no sign that she did, for she stayed bent to her work the whole while, moving slowly along the rows, her hoe rising and falling, chopping weeds, rising and falling, and it seemed he could feel the blistery heat of the wood handle in his own palms. He touched his heels to the horse's ribs and rode it forward until she stood and turned and looked at him, the hoe raised ready to chop another patch of weeds from the unforgiving earth.

"*Hola, amiga,*" he said, for he could not tell for certain if she was Mexican or Indian or maybe a little of both.

She was maybe as old as he, her face the color of tarnished copper. He hair was long and black and twisted in a ponytail that hung down her back like a frayed rope and she wore a straw hat, not unlike his own. She looked at him with unflinching eyes. She didn't say anything at first.

He removed his hat and wiped his forehead with the back of his wrist, realizing he must have presented a rough appearance to her.

"I am *Señor* Juárez," he said, leaning forward in the saddle with his hands resting on the horn. He made an effort to smile to let her know he was just a simple man that didn't want to visit any harm on her.

"What you want here, mister?" she said. Her voice was flat, the words clipped.

"You see," he began, "I have not eaten in three days." He held up three fingers.

She looked him over pretty well. "You're skinny," she said.

He nodded and looked down at himself. "I have to agree with you. I look like an old sack of bones."

"You Mexican?" she said.

He nodded.

"I'm part Mexican, part Apache," the woman said. "My old husband was Osage. He ran off two, three years ago. Had the drinking fever and ran off with a young Cherokee girl who had a clubfoot. Never did come back. He ever come back here, I'll shoot him. He wasn't never no good anyhow. I'm glad he run off. You want to get down?"

"Yes," Pablo said.

She told him her name was Rosemary.

"That's a good name," Pablo said, repeating it.

"You want to eat some squash with me?" she asked.

"Yes. I'd like to eat some squash."

"My corn ain't ready yet," she said.

"That's OK."

"I got a little meat . . . some salted pork."

"No, the squash will be fine."

He sat under a little *ramada* there in the shade and drank some *tizwin* she offered him. He'd drunk the Apache beer before, down along the border. It was bitter but slaked his thirst; the woman kept it cooled in *ollas* hanging there under the *ramada*. He watched as she cooked the squash and fried some bread. She smoked a pipe as she worked.

"I like tobacco," she said, when she saw him staring at her.

"I never bothered with it much," he said.

"It's pretty good."

He ate the squash and three or four of the fry breads she made and washed it down with some more of the *tizwin*.

"What you doing clear out here?" she asked.

"I'm looking for someone."

"Who?"

"Some men."

"Why you looking for them?"

"They killed my wife."

"Oh, that's too bad. You looking for a new wife, too?"

"No. I guess I'm not. Not too many women would put up with me. I got some bad ways."

She laughed. "I got my bad ways, too," she said.

He nodded.

She looked him over, appraising him, his condition, his age. "How many are these men you're looking for?"

"*Cinco* . . . five," he said.

She squinted over the pipe smoke. "Too many for just one man."

"Maybe. Maybe not."

"You're kinda old, eh?"

He shrugged.

"What if you catch them and they kill you?"

"Then I guess that will be the end of it for me."

"You ought not go after them," she said.

"I think it is going to rain soon," he said.

"Yes, I think so, too." She looked up at the sky, then back at him.

The warm sun ahead of the storm, along with the *tizwin* had made him drowsy. "How do you make it here alone, since your husband ran off and left you? This looks like some pretty poor ground."

"I can raise enough in my garden, long as I keep at the weeds," she said. "I have a few chickens. I used to have a cow, but she went dry and wouldn't give me no more milk, so I sold her."

"Why didn't you just butcher and eat her?"

"I had that cow a long time. I don't guess I could just eat her. I wish I still had her. She was a good cow."

"I know. You have something with you a long time and then, when it's gone, you miss it."

"Yes."

She resumed smoking her pipe. He felt the weariness of a long journey and a full belly and the opiate of the *tizwin* settle into his marrow. He closed his eyes, heard the slight sucking sound the woman made smoking the pipe, felt the warm air being swept along before the coming storm.

"You're pretty wore out, eh?"

"Yes," he said, opening his eyes. "I've ridden a long way."

"You want to sleep a little?"

"Sometimes, when I sleep, I dream of my wife."

"I don't never dream of my old husband," she said, grinning broadly. "But sometimes I dream of young men coming to my bed."

He looked at her, saw the devilment in her eyes. "I don't have any money to pay you for the meal."

She stopped puffing. "Who asked you to pay, eh?"

"I would like to pay you for your kindness."

"Ah, squash don't cost hardly nothing." Then she settled back to smoking her pipe again.

In the distance they could hear the rumble of thunder behind the amassing cloud heads.

"It looks like it might be a pretty big storm," he said.

"Once a storm came and the wind blew the roof off the house. It blew away some of my chickens, too. I never did find them. I hope this storm don't blow away the rest of my chickens."

"I remember one time in Texas that it rained so much, some of the horses drowned," he said.

"That must have been some pretty bad storm."

"It was a sad thing to see all those drowned horses."

"You better go sleep in the house," she said. "Or you might drown like them horses did."

"I should keep riding."

"If you did, maybe you *would* drown. Can't you see how big those clouds are?"

"Maybe I'll sleep for just a little while . . . just until the storm passes."

"Sure, you better do that."

He was grateful to her, more than he could say. She had the same kindness as his María. She showed him a place where he could lay down inside the house; it was near a window in a small room off the kitchen.

"This is where my old husband would sleep when we weren't getting along too good," she said, pointing toward the pallet on the floor. "He slept there a lot."

The first drops of rain clicked against the window as he lay down upon the pallet. It felt good, being here, at rest, the rain dancing against the window above his head, its rhythm lulling him to sleep, the *tizwin* easing the dull ache in his bones.

He must have slept a long time, because when he awakened, the storm had passed and the sky was a dusty rose color and beyond the setting sun, the storm clouds glowed silver. It took him a moment to gather his wits about him and remember where he was. He found the woman sitting outside in the rain-washed air, smoking her pipe.

"*Hola*," he said.

"The storm knocked down all of my corn," she said.

He looked toward the garden. The stalks were lying over, their long waxy leaves in puddles of water. "I'm sorry."

"Me, too."

He suddenly felt angry, his head full of angry thoughts against God. Why was kindness always repaid with unkindness? Why did the men kill his wife after he'd offered them kindness? Why did the storm ruin this poor woman's corn? Maybe it was he that God was angry at for all those times when he was a bandit. Maybe that is what it was. God was paying him back for his sins. But why take it out on his wife and this woman simply because of their kindness toward him? He walked over and looked more closely at the broken stalks.

"It won't do no good to look at them," she said.

"I just wanted to see."

"Go ahead and look, then."

"I didn't even hear it," he said. "The storm."

"You were sleeping pretty good. Snoring. It was a pretty bad storm. I thought maybe it would take the roof off again and maybe some of my chickens. But the roof didn't go nowhere. Just the corn."

He felt ashamed for having slept through the storm.

"I still got some seed left," she said. "In the morning, I will plant the corn again."

He turned and looked at her. She seemed undisturbed by her loss. "It doesn't bother you?" he said. "Losing your corn?"

"Yes, but there is nothing I can do about it except plant some more. What else can I do about it?"

"I don't know."

"You see. It is like that sometimes. Things happen that you can't do nothing about. You just have to live with it."

"I will stay and help you plant the corn again," he said.

"I thought you were looking to find those men who killed your wife?"

"I still am. But another day won't make any difference. I don't even know where to look for them."

"It's a pretty big place, this country. I don't know how you are going to find a few men in such a big place."

"I don't know, either."

"You don't have to stay. I can plant the corn myself. I did it alone the last time."

"I will stay and help you."

"It's OK with me if you want to stay."

He didn't know any other way of repaying her kindness to him. He would still have plenty of time to find the men who killed his wife. What would one more day matter?

"I will fix a little meat and some bread for supper," she said.

He could see the sun now, descending beyond the woods, blood red against the black, wet trunks of the trees. He could hear the croaking of frogs beginning against the onset of night. Later, when he was eating the meat and some of the bread the old woman had fixed for their supper, he heard an owl calling.

The woman stopped eating just then.

"What?" he said.

"If you hear the owl call your name, it means you will die soon."

"Yes, I've heard that, too."

"Do you believe it?"

"I don't know. My wife used to tell me things like that. But I didn't know what to believe about them."

"There's some truth to what the Indian peoples know," she said. "But some of it is just talk."

"I know."

She still didn't eat anything more for a few minutes; she just sat there listening to see if the owl called again. After a while, she began to eat again, her eyes fixed to some uncertainty in her mind.

"You are a good cook," he said.

She laughed. "I bet my old husband misses it. He liked to eat and was big and fat. I hope that skinny girl he ran off with don't know how to cook. It will make him sorry he ran off from me."

She had a funny laugh and it caused him to smile. "It would serve him right if he was," Pablo said.

"I miss my people sometimes."

"Where are they?"

"Most of them went to Mexico after the Army chased them out of Arizona. They didn't have no choice but to go down there. I guess later some of them got to come back. But I think they were put on the reservation, some place called San Carlos."

"Why don't you go back if you miss them?"

"I don't know. It's been a long time since I seen any of them. You know how it is. Maybe, if I went to find them, it wouldn't be the same like it was, like I remember. I like it here. But I might like it there, too, if I was to go back. I think about it

119

sometimes."

"Well, you could go and see how it is, and then, if you liked it, you could stay there with your people. Wouldn't that be better than being here alone?"

She shrugged her shoulders. "Maybe."

He recognized the look of longing that swam in her eyes. He'd felt it, too, the wanting to go back to a time and place that was better than where he now found himself. Maybe someday he would; maybe someday they both would. But for now, he would help her replant the corn, and then he would go look for the men who killed his wife.

"You want some more meat?" she said.

"Sure."

CHAPTER SIXTEEN

There were two women and a fancily dressed man who was reading a small red book and they'd all looked up. The boy could see right away in their eyes they knew this was no ordinary business that was about to be conducted. They had arrived in the dark and they could see the lights of the building from a good distance and it felt a welcoming sight as it always did when he was hungry and riding half the night—to see lights in the dark.

Caddo had told them that he knew about this place, that a white man ran it and he had whores working for him. He said, too, that the man was probably dangerous in the extreme because rumor had it he had killed some men back East.

"Most of these whore men you got to watch out for. Let me do the talking," Caddo had said. "He might trust a white man more'n you *Indian* boys."

So that's the way it went. They had dismounted and gone in and the white man was sitting in a chair reading a book with the two women sitting on the floor near his feet. The white man looked up and acted as though nothing was wrong. But the boy could see the caution in his eyes. The white man stood up and walked behind the bar and poured them whiskey and talked to them, saying something to the effect that the girls didn't work on Sundays. The boy found it amazing that he had lost track of even what day it was. But time seemed to mean more to white men than it did to Indians. The two white men talked about it for a while. The boy and the others stood at the bar, drinking the man's liquor and looking at the women.

Then, after a time of talking, the man said that maybe if they were to come back the next day they could do some business as far as the women were concerned, and Caddo had tried stringing the man along, saying how they had a lot of distance to cover and he and the Indian boys had come a long distance out of their way to do some business tonight and not tomorrow.

The white man tried being clever about it, making his movements seem casual behind the bar while he poured the whiskey. Then Billy Starr walked up behind him while he was talking to Caddo and shot the man in the head, causing a splatter of blood and bone that flew into Caddo's face and caused him to step back with a start and say: "God damn, Billy!"

"What you think, you were going to talk that fool to death?" Billy said, looking down at his handiwork before reaching in the man's pocket and retrieving the red book.

The rest of them had nearly jumped out from under their hats when Billy's pistol exploded and the two women screamed.

Billy stood there looking at the book for a moment before tossing it to the floor, and the boy saw that there were bloodstains on it that were darker red than the leather covers and there was a small tongue of red ribbon hanging from its pages. Caddo had wiped the white man's blood from his face with the back of his hand and looked at it, then said to Billy Starr, if he ever did a dirty trick like that again, they might have some real trouble between them. Billy gave him a hard, challenging stare but said nothing. Caddo knew the boy wanted to fight him for control of the gang, but he was determined the boy would burn in hell first. One of them sure would.

The book on the floor reminded Red Snake of some early childhood memory that was unclear but one he remembered that had to do with books. He picked it up and put it into his pocket when the others had turned their attention to the women. Later, when he stood watch near the corral, he took the book from his pocket and tilted the pages toward the wan light coming from the cabin's windows. And as his finger traced the lines of print, he heard the raucous sounds coming from within the cabin and tried to close his ears to it, just as he had the other times. The book and the fragmented memory that the book raised and the presence of horses and moonlight had stirred something in him that had been long missing. Then the wind came and spoke to him and told him that he was the child of a star that had fallen to earth in the form of a woman.

The wind said: "Your blood flows yet in this woman and in the man who found her after she'd fallen to earth." Then it blew through the dark and passed in front of the moon before ruffling the pages of the book. The printed words were a mystery to Red Snake. A chill passed through him from front to back, like the passing of a steel blade through his body. Then he heard one of the women cry out from inside the cabin, followed by a silence so harsh that not even the wind could break it.

Red Snake awakened to what he thought was a dream. But then he saw that the dream was real, that fog had crept in during the night and blanketed everything. He was cold and stiff from having spent the night there by the corral, sleeping with his back against a gnarled blackjack post.

He was still unraveling himself from his dreams when one of the horses nickered and was answered by another, farther off, from somewhere near the woods. He thought he saw movement in the mist. He hurried inside the cabin and told the others, and they quickly grabbed up their rifles and pistols and took up positions by the windows.

He saw the two women in the corner of the room, blankets wrapped around them, their eyes red and troubled. The younger of the two stared silently, while the other looked at him defiantly and he felt her defiance burn the side of his face.

Billy Starr ordered him and Jamoa July to go to the privy and take up positions there, stating that whoever was outside could be caught in a crossfire between the privy and the cabin if they were to ride in. Jamoa complained and Billy struck him across the cheek with the barrel of his pistol, drawing a welt of blood.

Red Snake went to the privy with Jamoa still touching his busted cheek, and they stood inside with the door partially ajar while Jamoa complained of the poor treatment Billy had shown him, saying: "I'm just the god-damn' same as him. I'm a god-damn' Creek and so's he. Where's he get the right hitting me in the god-damn' face like that?"

They stood there, listening and smelling the stink that came up from the sit holes and mixed with the metallic fog.

"You think there's somebody out there, Snake?" Jamoa asked worriedly. And when Red Snake shrugged and said he didn't know, Jamoa said: "Have to be. If it was just somebody riding through, innocent, they'd been here by now. Have to be the god-damn' law, don't you think?"

Then they heard the riders and Jamoa said: "Shit, here they come!"

Chapter Seventeen

They came through the fog. Jimmy Wild Bird checked his horse and said in a low voice: "There it is."

The grayish outline of a building stood, ghostly and silent, perhaps a hundred yards distant and there was an uncanny quiet there in the woods where they sat their horses.

"You think we beat 'em here?" Joe Digger asked.

"Hard to tell," Jimmy said. "The way this fog is, there could be horses down there, maybe not."

"We ride in, or what?"

"We could, or we could sit and wait for it to burn off." The lawman looked at John Henry Cole. "What do you think?"

"I don't like going in blind," Cole said.

The fog lay around them like wet smoke and you could hear water dripping off the leaves of the scrub oak and you could almost taste the air, wet and cool as it was.

Jimmy pulled a fat pocket watch from his coat and snapped open the face and said: "It's seven-fifteen."

"Maybe they're there," Digger said. "We'll kill 'em eatin' breakfast."

"I don't want them killed," Jimmy said.

"You might not have no choice, Constable."

Cole shucked the Winchester from its boot and checked the breech, then rested it across the pommel. "I vote to wait," he said. "Least until we can get the lay of things."

Digger dismounted and tightened his cinch strap.

"They could be waiting right inside," Jimmy said, "or we might have gotten here first."

They'd ridden hard and with little rest, cutting across country, but it was no assurance that they'd reached Greasy Junction before the renegades. The trouble with hunting men was, you never knew which way they were going to jump because they never knew which way *they* were going to jump. So sitting there in the fog, waiting for the sun to rise high enough to burn things off, none of them could be certain their quarry was in the bush.

Digger pulled a bottle of whiskey from his saddlebags.

"Leave off with that," Cole said.

Digger looked hard at Cole, defiantly took a quick pull, then slipped the bottle back into his saddlebags. "A man needs breakfast," was all he said.

Jimmy had also dismounted and was pouring water from his canteen into a cupped hand for his horse to drink when a horse nickered through the bank of fog and Jimmy's mount raised its head and answered.

"If they're down there, they know we're here," Cole said.

"Then I say to hell with it, let's ride down and find out," Jimmy said, throwing himself into leather.

"Hold on," Cole said, but it was too late. Jimmy had put spurs to his horse and was gone through the fog.

"What the hell . . . ?" Digger said.

"Let's go!" Cole said, and slapped the rump of his pony with the barrel of the Winchester.

It was like riding into a nightmare, one of those you have where you're in danger and blind and can feel deep down in your gut that there's nothing you can do but pray a bullet doesn't find you before you wake up. In the rush and confusion and fog, they got separated. It was as though the fog simply swallowed them up when they rode into it. You couldn't see more distance than a good spit in front of you.

Cole came busting out of the woods and down the slight slope to where the cabin sat just in time to catch glimpse of the tail end of the two riders ahead of him. Then, as if commanded by some higher power, the fog cleared right there in front of the cabin and Jimmy and Joe Digger appeared as if by magic. Cole could see there were horses in the corral, at least seven horses by quick count, and some were still saddled.

The first gunshot buckled the front legs of Jimmy's horse and for a moment he seemed suspended in mid-flight before hitting the ground in a tumble. Digger pulled his animal up short but already too late as they opened up. A bullet tore away Cole's right stirrup and he saw Digger twist hard in his saddle as if from a blow. Jimmy had regained his feet and was firing both his pistols at the cabin while trying to duck-walk his way to a water trough to the west of the cabin.

Cole slapped the reins against the withers of his mount, then saw Digger snatched from his saddle as though an invisible rope had snagged him. He landed hard, rolled over, and got to his hands and knees, coughing up blood.

There was a lot of gunfire and it wasn't all coming from the cabin. Cole saw a rifle barrel poking from the door of a privy and fired a round through it and jacked the lever of the Winchester, and fired again. Wood splintered and a body tumbled halfway out.

Cole spurred his mount to reach Digger, who had gotten to one knee. Cole could see Digger'd been shot in the arm and side; blood drenched his shirt. Cole reached for Digger, bringing himself and horse between Digger and the cabin. Cole held out his hand to pull Digger aboard when something hot drove into his leg. His horse jumped away, the bullet having gone through Cole's leg muscle and punched into the gelding's ribs, sending it into a panic.

Digger fell flat trying to reach Cole's hand, righted himself, gave Cole a hard look, then the top of his head exploded and his body arched as though struck by a lightning bolt, before toppling backward. A bullet clipped Cole's hat and another struck the horn of his saddle. Cole jerked his self-cocker and rapid-fired at the cabin as he leaned low over his pony's neck and jumped the water trough. He could see Jimmy Wild Bird's elbow blown out from a round; pieces of ivory bone and bloody torn flesh poked through his shirt sleeve. The arm hung limply at his side.

"Climb up!" Cole shouted, reaching for him.

He shook his head. "They've killed us!"

"Not yet, they haven't. Climb up!"

He reached his good arm for Cole, then a fusillade hit Cole's horse, toppling it over. Cole leaped free, tumbled along the ground, then scrabbled behind the trough where Jimmy now lay, staring at his shattered elbow. Cole could hear bullets slapping the water above their heads and thunking into the boards of the trough.

"Jesus Christ," Jimmy muttered. "Jesus Christ."

"We'll make the woods," Cole said.

"What about Digger?"

"He's killed."

"We'll die, too, we try crawling out from behind this trough."

"We'll sure as hell die if we stay."

Cole saw the fear in his eyes, the doubt that every man has to face at one point or another in his life. Even in the best of them, Cole had seen that look. At Shiloh and Pea Ridge and a dozen other places, he'd seen that look. He'd had that look in his own eyes more than once. You tell yourself you're too young to die, that you're not ready, that it can't be happening to you. You tell yourself lots of things, but nothing works, and the fear rises up from your gut and the bile catches in your throat. "Get moving," Cole said. "I'll lay down a covering fire." Jimmy looked again at his elbow. "Move, god damn it!"

The only thing that lay between them and the woods was an old tool shed, but they had the fog that was still dense away from the house, and if they could reach the shed, they could slither off into the fog, then the woods beyond. Cole shoved the self-cocker into his belt and took up the Winchester once again and began laying down rapid fire into the cabin. Jimmy broke cover, and Cole thought maybe they would make it, then he heard Jimmy cry out and turned in time to see him go down. Cole yelled for him to get up, but he barely moved.

Cole kept up the fire until the hammer fell with a metallic snap. He reloaded the self-cocker, took the hide-out Colt Lightning from the shoulder rig. Twelve chances to save them, six rounds of lead in each pistol. He fired all twelve, then broke for Jimmy, grabbed him by the belt, and hauled him toward the tool shed.

The bullets split the air like killer bees but with every foot of ground Cole gained, their luck increased and his heart was pumping blood so hard he barely felt the hole in his leg. They landed behind the tool shed with a thump with bullets clanging off a rusted anvil, but they had made it.

"How bad you hit?" Cole inquired.

Jimmy rolled over. The bullet had caught him in the back, but low, beneath the ribs. "I'm a damn' fool," he said.

"Don't remind me." The color had washed out of him. "We got to make those woods," Cole said.

Jimmy shook his head. "You go on, leave me."

"You're not dead yet."

"I will be."

"Only if you stay here."

"I ain't afraid of dying," he said.

"Well, I am. Now grab hold."

Cole picked him up and put him across his shoulders. He wasn't that large a man. The fire from the cabin had ceased and Cole could see that the sun was getting high enough that it was beginning to burn off the rest of the fog. They had to make the woods at least. There they could make a last stand of it if they had to.

Cole's leg was starting to hurt now as he carried Jimmy, and Cole could feel the blood filling up his boot. It was a warm mushy feeling that quickly turned to a cold mushy feeling as the blood leaked out. His leg grew colder and more painful, the blood taking vital heat with it.

They finally made the tree line, and in a half dozen paces Cole dropped to the ground and rolled Jimmy off his shoulders, both of them breathing hard. Jimmy lay on his back, looking up through the trees at the fog-shrouded sun. Cole took off his bandanna and plugged the hole in his thigh muscle with it. Then he took off Jimmy's bandanna and tied it around his elbow, and Jimmy winced when he did it as if he'd been touched with a hot iron. Cole looked again at the puckered wound below Jimmy's ribs. Like Cole, he'd been lucky that the shot had gone clean through. Cole took off Jimmy's belt and strapped it around his upper waist—the tail of his dirty shirt being the only bandage there was—and then leaned back, trying hard to catch his breath.

Jimmy lay there like a wounded animal, breathing hard and staring at the hazy sky, the shrouded sun. "You think they'll come?" he said.

"They'd be fools to come walking up to these woods."

"No they wouldn't, look at us . . . shot to pieces, shot up as sin."

"We may have got a few of them as well," Cole said. "I dropped one in the privy."

Jimmy blinked the sweat out of his eyes. "I don't know what got into me," he said. "I just so god-damn' bad wanted them, I didn't want them to get away. . . ."

"Well, they sure as hell didn't get away," Cole said as he took out the makings and fashioned a cigarette and lit it. He offered it to Jimmy.

Shaking his head, Jimmy said: "Tobacco and whiskey were never my vices."

"Tell me, if I had a bottle of Digger's Tennessee whiskey right now, you wouldn't take a drink."

He exhaled. "I'd drink every god-damn' drop," he said.

"So would I."

Cole reloaded his pistols and the one Jimmy carried in a cross-over holster, and then counted the number of shells they had left between them. Twenty-one chances to live.

"What now?" Jimmy said.

"We wait."

"Till they come?"

"Till they come or decide to get in the wind."

"I can't feel my hand," Jimmy said.

Cole looked at the shattered elbow, the bandanna already soaked with blood, dark and red. "You able to shoot either hand?" he asked.

Jimmy nodded.

"Then I wouldn't worry about it too much."

Jimmy looked away, but Cole could see the bitterness in his eyes. The arm would never be any good to him any more. It's hard to lose a piece of yourself and not feel bitter. It takes time for the reality of it to settle in. Then it never does completely.

"I wouldn't worry about that arm so much," Cole repeated.

Jimmy looked at him. "It ain't so much that."

"What, then?"

"We didn't finish the job, is what it is," he said. "I'd lose an arm *and* a leg if I had to, just to bring those bastards in."

"Hell, I don't know so much about that."

"Was you me, you'd understand," he said.

"Was I you, maybe so. But look at it this way . . . at least you've lived to fight those boys another day."

He winced, coughed, and shook his head. "We need to finish it," he said.

"You suggesting we go back and let them have another crack at us?"

"No. Not now."

"Appreciate it," Cole said. "This is the seventh time I've been shot since I became a man. Not one time has it felt good. I don't feature carrying any more lead around in me."

"We might both be dead by sunset," Jimmy said almost casually, like it wouldn't matter one way or the other.

They waited all that day, and into the evening. Then they heard running horses.

"You hear that?" Jimmy asked.

"They got in the wind."

"Shit. . . ."

Cole looked at Jimmy in the fading light and thought to himself that he'd never known another man so all determined to do his job even if it cost him an arm or his life. "We'll get another chance at them," he said.

"How do you know?"

"Just a feeling, Jimmy. Just a real bad feeling."

CHAPTER EIGHTEEN

For five days Pablo stayed with the woman. He helped her plant corn and harvested some of the squash and checked the progress of the beans and peppers. At the end of each day, they sat and talked into the evenings and drank *tizwin* and Rosemary smoked her pipe and asked Pablo questions about himself and told him about herself and her people and what it was to be of mixed blood: half Indian, half Mexican.

"Be glad you aren't cursed like me," she said one evening.

"How do you mean, cursed?"

"Half of this, half of that don't make you a whole of nothing."

On the morning of the sixth day, he grew restless. "I am going," he said.

"Why don't you stay?"

"It would be easier. But I told you, I have to go find those men and kill them."

"Maybe you go and maybe you don't ever find them," she said. "Then what?"

"Oh, I'll find them. I've found lots of men like them when I was younger."

"You were a pretty bad man in them days, huh?"

"Yes, I was a bad *hombre*."

"Then that's it, you're going to go off. You think maybe someday you'll come back up this way?"

"I don't know," he said. "Maybe those men will kill me. But

if they don't, maybe I'll come back. I still have to take that horse back to the man I borrowed him from."

The sky looked bruised and a cool wind blew down from the north. She watched him go out to the shed and begin to saddle his horse. She felt sorry for him, an old man like that riding around the country looking for men to kill. He should be sitting somewhere, drinking coffee or a little liquor and telling lies about his life.

She went in the house and fixed him a sack of food, some beef jerky and biscuits and an *olla* of *tizwin* he could take with him. A man shouldn't go out in the world hungry or thirsty. She took a spare blanket from the bed and took these things out to him.

"Here," she said. "A little something to make your journey comfortable."

He looked at her from across the seat of his saddle. "You want me to kill that husband of yours if I come across him?" he asked.

She laughed. They both did.

"Naw, don't waste no good bullets on someone like him."

"OK," he said, and swung up into the saddle and adjusted his old hat, pulling up the stampede string tight under his chin.

"I see him, I'll just scare him a little."

She held the reins of his horse until he looked down at her with that determined gaze she'd come to like. "*Adiós,*" he said.

"Maybe I'll see you sometime."

"*Sí,* maybe so."

She watched him turn the horse back up toward the road, and then ride it at a canter like he and his horse were one creature. *You sure must've been something, mister, when you was a young man! Look at the way you sit up on that fine horse so proud and stiff like you own all the world, like all the world is going to know who you are when you come riding through. Ha! I bet all the women were after you in them days when you was a young man!*

When he had ridden out of sight, she said to the wind: "You ain't coming back, old man, just like my old husband never came back. Men leave, they don't come back. Only I don't miss him for nothing. But I sure might miss you."

Pablo could feel the old woman's eyes on him as he rode away. He hated to leave her in a way, but his business wasn't finished, and until it was, he had no room in his heart for anyone or anything. He rode east for a while, then south. The direction he should ride wasn't firm in his mind. One way seemed as good as another. Perhaps he would come across someone who had heard of the men he was looking for. If he continued to ride back and forth, in different directions all the time, the chances were pretty good he might hear something, might meet someone who knew about the men and could tell him where they were.

That night he camped by some rocks and a small stream, and, as the darkness fell around him, he felt a lot lonelier than he had the last several nights. He thought of the old woman smoking her pipe, looking at him through eyes of disappointment. He heard an owl hoot off in one of the trees and remembered what the old woman said. Then he thought he should think of her as Rosemary and not just as the old woman. He wondered if the owl was calling his name now from up in that tree. *Hooo, hooo.* It sure didn't sound like his name.

He tried not to think about her too much. But it was a hard thing not to do, looking up at the sky flung with stars and feeling like the last man on earth, like God had dropped him here in the middle of nowhere to be by himself all the rest of his days. *I think maybe you are watching me, eh, to see which way I jump . . . like a frightened rabbit, or like a man. But it don't matter that you are watching me, because I ain't afraid. And when you let those men kill my Maria, well, you had to know I would take care of this business you put in front of me.*

Then he saw a single star shoot across the sky like an unanswered prayer and he closed his eyes and tasted the bitterness of his sorrow before falling asleep like a fallen angel in repose.

CHAPTER NINETEEN

They slept in blood. Several times during the night John Henry
Cole awoke from dreams in which a man stood over him, his
pistol aimed at Cole's face, his laughter like the ripping of cloth
as Cole watched his finger squeeze the trigger. Cole would
awake, feel the pain in his leg, the cold wetness of blood in his
boot, and remember the shooting. The darkness of the night
was complete—no moon, a clouded sky blotting out even the
stars. It was as if he had been dropped down a deep hole in the
earth, and it was a fearful place to be.

Cole managed to shake the shroud of dread and bring himself
fully awake. He rolled a shuck and smoked it. Only the rasping
breathing of Jimmy Wild Bird told Cole that Jimmy was still
alive. He wouldn't be for long if Cole didn't find some help.
Cole knew the wound Jimmy had suffered to his elbow, if left
untreated, would turn to gangrene and the poisoned blood
would flow to his heart and that would be the end of him. Cole
had seen it happen before—during the war, men with relatively
minor wounds that turned their blood to poison and stilled
their hearts.

The smoke brought a sort of peace and gave Cole a chance
to rein in his thoughts. He remembered horses running, the
stifled moans of the Indian, night descending, sleep. Something
walked in the woods, a twig snapped, and Cole stiffened before
realizing it wasn't the footfall of a man but probably a raccoon
or opossum and eased the hammer back down on his pistol. He

took a deep draw on the shuck, then heard another sound, a long wailing like the cry of a panther and realized it was coming from the cabin and that it was human.

Cole moved to the side of the policeman and shook him awake, clamping his hand over Jimmy's mouth as he did. "There's someone still in the cabin," he said. "Don't talk but stay alert, if you can. I'm going down to take a look."

Cole felt the fever of Jimmy's flesh against his palm; the poison was already starting to gather itself in his blood. Cole's leg was stiff and hurt like there was a wedge of cold steel driven into it, but he could walk well enough and he made his way to the cabin, sensing every step, feeling his way, holding his every breath.

He got close, saw the frame of greasy, yellow light in the window, and his heart quickened. The wailing sound that had caught his attention had stopped. The cabin was now as silent as the night. He saw the women through the window—one lying on the bed, the other sitting next to her, holding her hand. The cabin's light played far enough out into the yard that Cole could see that the horses in the corral were gone. He saw the boots of a man, sticking out from behind a counter at the opposite end of the room, the toes pointing skyward.

The woman sitting up looked at Cole when he walked in. "Jesus!" was all that she said. It was more a rasp than a spoken word.

Cole quickly checked behind the counter, saw the dead man, half his face blown away. Then he saw that the woman lying on the bed had a crimson flower of blood staining her bodice just above the heart.

"Who are you?" the woman sitting next to the bed said.

Cole told her his name and asked her if she was hurt.

"I thought you were one of them come back," she said.

"I ain't."

"They killed Mister Saint John and Pleasure," she said, looking at the woman on the bed.

"When did they leave and which direction did they go?"

She shook her head. "Sometime earlier. I don't know."

Cole wondered why they'd left her alive but didn't ask. "I have a friend bad shot, out in the woods," he said. "I could use your help getting him."

She wasn't an unattractive woman, but Cole could see that whatever years she'd spent on the frontier had been hard ones for her. She looked at him with a gaze that was resigned, as though she'd seen what was waiting for her at the end of the line and had accepted it. "Too much killing," she said.

"I won't disagree with you," Cole said.

She lowered her gaze, then took the woman's limp hand she'd been holding and placed it across the dead woman's waist, and stood up. The dead woman was younger, pretty, peaceful in repose. Her friend brushed away strands of hair that had come loose and hung in reddish tendrils about her face like winter-scarred ivy. "The Indians wanted to cut my throat," she said. "The white man wanted to cut out my tongue so I wouldn't tell on them."

Cole saw a shawl hanging on a door peg and put it around her shoulders. "I could use your help getting my friend."

Cole found a lantern and lit it, and they went out and found Jimmy in the woods, and together managed to get him back to the cabin.

"If you'll strip off his clothes and tend to his wounds," Cole said, "I'll take your friends outside and bury them."

She didn't say anything for a long time, then began to strip off Jimmy's clothes.

Cole carried out the dead and laid them next to the body of Joe Digger. Then he found the Indian boy in the privy and carried him out and laid him next to the other three. He smoked a shuck and caught his wind, then went and found a shovel, and dug graves until the light dawned gray in the east and his shirt was soaked with sweat. He rolled the bodies into the graves and smoked another shuck before finishing the task of burying them.

When he finished and went inside the cabin, the woman had Jimmy lying beneath clean sheets. A pan of bloody water rested on a night table; bloody rags lay piled on the floor. Cole found a chair and sat at the table, and the woman brought a pot of coffee she had boiling on the stove and set two tin cups on the table and filled them and took a seat across from him.

"You look done in," she said.

Cole sipped the coffee and took the makings out and spilled tobacco trying to roll a shuck. She took the makings and said: "Here, let me." She rolled a cigarette for each of them and then lit them with a sulphur match that she struck off a nail head in the table.

Cole watched her as he drank his coffee and she watched him. She had eyes as blue as worn denim. Cole could see the bruises on her cheek and along her neck. Some looked like bite marks. He tried not to think what the renegades had put her through. Maybe her friend was the lucky one. She wouldn't have to remember; she wouldn't have to forget.

"They were my family," she said, the cigarette smoke wreathing her face.

"I'm sorry."

"For what? You didn't kill them."

Cole took a draw from the smoke. "You know of any doctors nearby?"

She shook her head. "Might be one or two in Tulsa," she said. "But Tulsa's a two-day ride from here. I doubt your friend will make it two days. He's burning up with fever."

Cole noticed the zinc tub in the corner. "We'll fill that with cold water," he said. "Put him in it. It might break the fever."

"He'll surely die."

"He surely will if we do nothing."

"I've seen all the dead men I want to," she said.

"You'll see one more if we don't break his fever."

Cole hauled water in buckets from a nearby well that ran, deep and cold, and once he had the zinc tub filled, they lifted Jimmy Wild Bird and sank him to his armpits in it. He moaned and shook like a sick dog, but they held him down until he stopped shaking. He gritted his teeth and his eyes rolled up white in his head. They fed him whiskey with a spoon and rubbed a pumice stone over him until his flesh looked raw and the water itself turned warm from his fever. Then they hauled him out and dried him and wrapped him in blankets, and placed him back in the bed.

It was exhausting labor and Cole soon found himself dozing in the chair, and the woman made a pallet on the floor and said: "Why don't you lay down and get some sleep?" Cole looked at her and she said: "If you can't trust me now, you might as well shoot me." He laid down and closed his eyes and could feel his senses being snatched away.

Cole awoke once to see the woman kneeling over him, washing his leg with cool water and wrapping it with a clean white bandage, and her hands were like balm. How long he slept altogether he couldn't say, except the shadows were long from the sun lying low, splayed out across the land, and he could see swallows darting through the trees, black and swift against the silver sky.

The woman sat on the edge of the porch, her elbows resting on her knees. She turned when Cole came out. "Thank you for what you did," he said.

"What choice did I have?"

"You want to tell me about it . . . what those men did to you and your friend?"

Bill Brooks

She looked at Cole from the corner of her eye as he sat next to her. "No, I don't want to talk about it. I learned a long time ago to trust men to act like dogs, given the opportunity."

"Why didn't they cut out your tongue so you wouldn't talk, or cut your throat?"

Her hard-eyed stare softened. She shook her head. "There was this one, just a boy, who stopped them."

"Then you were lucky."

"He told them he had a vision that whatever they did to me would be done to them."

"Indians are big on bad medicine," Cole said.

She nodded. "They were pretty well drunk at the time and had been talking among themselves. It seemed to have an effect on them . . . except for the white man, who wanted to cut me anyway, but the others wouldn't let him after the boy told them about the vision."

"They believe in spirits and a hereafter," Cole said.

"I never used to, but maybe I do now, a little," she said. "I think maybe I believe in those things, too."

"Why'd they kill your friends?"

"Mister Saint John. . . . They just did. One walked up and shot him. Pleasure was an accident, a stray bullet came through the window. She lived through what they done to her only to die like that. . . ."

The thought occurred to Cole that maybe it had been his bullet that had killed the woman and it cut him like sharp glass. They sat there for a time in the gloaming light.

"Will you take me away from here?" she said after a time.

"We have no horses."

"Then I guess I'll walk."

"Where?"

"It doesn't matter."

"You'd be taking a big risk. A woman alone, on foot."

142

"My whole life's been one big risk, Mister Cole. I reckon if I'm not dead by now, nothing out there is going to kill me."

"Stay for a time until I can figure something out."

"The swallows . . . ," she started to say, then lowered her face to her hands and wept.

Later she looked at Cole in the fading light and said: "Your eyes, there is something familiar about them."

"What?" Cole asked.

"I don't know, but I think I've seen them before."

CHAPTER TWENTY

They squatted in a cave and listened to water drip in the dark bowels of stone and were restless with fear, brooding, confusion. The attack had come unexpectedly and Billy Starr had questioned the white man, Caddo Pierce, about his earlier assertion that the white judge in Fort Smith would not send his deputies down on them, for until now they had not committed any crimes against whites.

Caddo's features were knotted with his own brand of fear and uncertainty, knowing that this young wolf was constantly on the prowl to attack him, make him look weak in the eyes of the others. His eyes shone wetly in the small light from the fire they'd built on the floor of the cave. He must not show them any weakness or they would attack, led by Billy Starr. He'd have to kill the boy, Red Snake, before it was all said and done.

Red Snake saw drawings on the walls that looked like riders on horses turned upside down, like buffalo running, like a rain of arrows, like a floating serpent. He had heard about such drawings from his grandfather, who told him that the ancient ones had lived in caves and had painted their stories on the walls and that such places were as sacred as the places where the dead were buried.

"Well, what about this?" Billy demanded. "How come those deputies come after us?"

"How the hell am I supposed to know?" Caddo snarled the words like a cur dog. "Maybe they wasn't deputies. Maybe the judge done gone and violated the law."

But this answer didn't appease Billy and he drew his pistol and aimed it at the face of Caddo Pierce and told him to get down on his knees, that he was going to shoot him.

The drawings seemed to move beneath the flickering light and the sound of water dripping in the darkness made the boy certain that they were in a sacred place and he said: "We are in the mouth of the first woman, ready to be swallowed if we are not careful."

Billy Starr turned on him, aimed his pistol at him, and said: "Shut the god-damn' hell up!"

But by this time the boy had given himself over to his visions and knew that whatever would be would be and that neither his will nor anyone else's could change matters—that his death, or his life, was not in any one of their hands, that if Billy Starr pulled the trigger, then that is what the higher power had willed. "This is a sacred place," he said. "Can't you feel the breath of the Great Mother?"

Billy turned and fired into the long darkness where the sound of dripping water came from. One, two, three times he fired and the shots flashed from his gun, creating a brightness that was as quick and hot as lightning. Then the ricocheting sound evaporated to silence, and in the blackness it was as though the Great Mother had swallowed Billy's bullets. And still the water dripped like unwelcome rain.

"You see," the boy said to Billy. "You have no power in this place."

Billy placed the end of his pistol's barrel against the temple of the boy and thumbed back the hammer; there was a double clicking sound as the hammer latched into place and the cylinder turned a single notch. "I have the power to blow out your brains," he said. "I have the power to kill you dead."

"Yes, you can kill me, but can you kill the flight of birds, or the dreams of the dead?"

The boy saw a look of uncertainty come into the eyes of Billy Starr as he slowly lowered his pistol and said: "God damn all this crazy, shitting talk. Shut up!"

"There's no way those deputies are legal," Pierce claimed, having pulled his own pistol and aimed it at Billy. "Now, you want a shooting match, get to it! Otherwise, don't ever pull a fuckin' pistol on me again, Billy."

The white man could see Billy was unnerved by the crazy talk of the younger boy and by staring down the long lonesome of a pistol barrel. "Aw, shit and double shit," he said. "What we going to do now?"

"Let me god damn' think, will ya?" Caddo said. "I'll come up with somethin'."

That night, while the others slept curled near the fire with their hands pressed between their knees like lost and abandoned children, Red Snake sat at the mouth of the cave and called silently on the spirits to give him a sign. He closed his eyes and went deeply into his spirit and came back again, and when he opened his eyes, he saw a fire in the sky that burned up the stars and caused the moon to fall beyond the trees. A frog came and told him secrets and a wolf called his name three times.

The next morning Caddo said: "I have a plan that will take care of this business once and for all." Billy Starr asked him what it was, and he said: "We'll double back on them, catch them with their drawers down, and kill every fuckin' one of them!"

Billy Starr said: "That's your plan?"

"Yes, yes!" Caddo cried. "We'll track them down and kill them all just like we did with the Indian Police and the Light Horse. The last thing they'll expect is us to double back on 'em."

Billy snorted disdainfully and urinated into the fire. "Those white deputies ain't no chicken-shit Indian Police."

"No, listen," Caddo said. "We don't just hunt them down and kill them, we cut off their god-damn' heads and send them back to Judge Parker in Fort Smith."

Billy buttoned his pants and spat.

"Send him the heads," Caddo said. "His deputies see that, they won't a one of them dare cross the river to come lookin' for us."

"What kind of crazy shit is that?" Billy said.

"Nobody's ever thumbed their nose at Judge Parker," Caddo said. "And those god-damn' deputies see the heads we'll send 'em, they will be scared shitless."

"Maybe it will just make them god-damn' mad," Billy said.

"No, they ain't no different than anybody else," Caddo said.

"What you boys think?" Billy said, asking Red Snake and Charley Fast Elk, who had been silent as stone since the shoot-out.

Charley nodded his head. "I'm for it, Billy."

"Snake?"

The boy didn't say anything; he already knew the answer.

Billy turned to face the white man there in the dancing flames of light that scored the older man's features in shadow and light. "We don't even know how many there are."

"It don't matter. Last thing they'll be expectin' is for us to turn the tables on them. 'Sides, I know we shot a couple of them sons-a-bitches. I seen 'em go down."

"Track 'em . . . ?" Billy said, as though weighing the consideration.

"Track 'em down and cut off their heads."

"Sure, why not."

And so it was decided that they would find the deputies, kill them, cut off their heads, and send them to Fort Smith.

The boy smiled. There were forces at work none but he knew

about, that none could control. They were as children being guided by the invisible hand of the Great Mother. She would lead them to slaughter and anoint their heads with blood. And when last he looked, the light of the sun had crept into the cave and crawled along the walls and shone brightly on the blood-red figures of upside-down riders, buffalo running, a rain of arrows, and floating serpents.

"We'll kill them all!" Billy yelped.

"We'll god-damn' kill everyone," Caddo said.

"And cut off their heads," Charley said.

Billy ran a finger across his throat and grinned like a demon the boy had seen once in his dreams. The demon had leathery wings and sharp claws and long teeth and his grandmother had to shake a rattle at it three times to chase it away. The boy silently began to sing his death song. He must prepare for what awaited them, the things he had witnessed in the burning sky the night the stars caught fire and the moon fell to earth. He sang of running buffalo and arrows of rain and riderless horses and the bite of serpents. He sang to the dead and asked them to prepare a place for him and he heard their voices rising up from the earth and the far places, saying: *Come, come, we will take you in and let you dwell among us.* And the leathery wings of death seemed to enfold him.

Caddo squatted on his haunches, sure he was going to have to kill Billy the first chance he got. The boy was getting way too aggressive toward him, and, if he didn't watch it, Billy would slip up in the middle of the night and slit his throat. He would have killed him then and there, as soon as he turned his back or squatted in the bushes with his drawers down around his ankles, but he needed every one of them until they could find those deputies and finish them off. It was puzzling to him how those deputies had got to be on their trail to start with. Until killing St. John, they had been careful about not breaking any laws for which Parker could send his men after them. He was too weary even to begin trying to figure out where they'd slipped up. Besides, he had his mind on a bank up in Kansas he planned to rob just as soon as they could find those deputies. First the law-men, then Billy, and he might just as well kill that stupid Charley and that crazy kid, Red Snake, while he was in a killing mood. *Next time you form yourself a gang, Caddo,* he told himself, *make sure it ain't got no damn' Indians and half-breeds in it. . . .*

Billy took Charley aside outside the cave, telling Caddo they were going to look after the horses, maybe scout up a rabbit or something to eat. As soon as they were out of earshot, Billy said: "We finish them deputies, I'm going to kill that old man."

Charley looked back toward the cave. "You going to start your own gang?"

"Yeah, you want to be in it?"

"Sure. What about Red Snake?"

Billy glanced over his shoulder to make sure the white man hadn't sauntered out of the cave to check on them. "We kill him, too.

Charley's eyes narrowed. "He's got white blood in him, remember. . . ."

"Kill all the white bloods," Billy said. "Every one of them. . . ."

★ ★ ★ ★ ★

Book IV

★ ★ ★ ★ ★

CHAPTER TWENTY-ONE

The woman awakened John Henry Cole and said: "Someone's coming."

Cole raised from the pallet, stiff and ungainly, and hobbled to the window. The brave new light of dawn splayed out across the eastern horizon and there, riding directly out of the bloody sun, was a man upon a wagon being pulled by a pair of mules. A whorl of dust rose behind the wagon and settled to earth again, golden and vaporous like a gilded cloud.

"It's a peddler of some sort," Cole reported.

She looked relieved. "Thank God, maybe we're saved."

Cole hitched up his galluses, tucked in his shirt, and brushed his hair under his hat before stepping outside. The air was clear and guileless. Across the road from the dug-out, wildflowers peeked from the grass like red and yellow butterflies come to rest. The new day felt bracing and the coming wagon did seem like a form of salvation if they were to have salvation at all.

The woman brought out a tin cup of coffee and handed it to Cole and said: "What do you think?"

"This is a hard land," Cole said, "full of hard types, and it wouldn't do to let our guard down."

As the wagon drew nearer, she said: "Why, he's an old colored man."

"If people get old on the frontier," Cole said, "it's because they're smarter and more canny than the rest of us."

She looked at Cole, then said: "I could care less how he got to be old. All I care about is he's got a wagon that can take us to Tulsa."

The man halted his team of mules just shy of what gallery there was in front of the dug-out. It was then Cole recognized him. He was the same man Jimmy, Joe Digger, and Cole had run into before, the one who told them about the Mexican. He sat there a time, looking at the place, the grass growing on the roof, the privy whose boards were shot full of holes, the four graves, Cole, the woman.

"Saw crows a mile back," he said. "Lots of 'em. Figured something bad happened to see that many crows all at once."

Inside the cabin, Jimmy coughed a racking cough and the woman slipped inside to check on him.

"Got somebody sick?" the man said.

"Shot," Cole said.

He nodded his head as though he already knew. "Bad place to get shot in . . . 'way out here."

"Your mules look thirsty," Cole said.

He looked at the well.

"Help yourself."

"Thank you."

Cole watched as he went over and filled the water bucket and brought it first to the off-hand mule, then refilled it for the other, holding the bucket as they lowered their muzzles and drank, their velvety ears twitching in the morning air. When he finished, he took off his hat and rubbed his forehead with the cuff of his shirt. "We met before," he said. "But I can't remember exactly where or when."

Cole told him.

"That's right, I remember now. You ever find Mister Juárez?"

Cole told him they hadn't.

"I see them graves is fresh," he said.

"We had some trouble."

"Just as I figured. You don't see that many crows together they ain't trouble some place nearby."

"I had a friend who believed the same thing," Cole said. "You a coffee drinker?"

"I am."

"Come on inside."

He followed Cole in, removing his hat as he did. He saw Jimmy lying on the bed in the corner but didn't comment, and instead took up a seat at the table. Cole poured him a cup of coffee. He drank some of it and looked at Cole with luminous eyes. His skin was as dark as polished walnut.

The woman brought them some corn cakes she'd baked in a pan, and the three sat and ate them and drank the coffee in nearly complete silence. Then Jimmy coughed and stirred and moaned. The man looked over again, then quickly looked away as though he ought not have looked in the first place.

"No chance you're a doctor?" Cole said.

He shook his head. "None whatsoever. I know how to doctor my mules and myself . . . but only if we ain't been shot."

"We'll need your help getting out of here, mister," the woman said.

He looked at her from across the table. "How you mean?"

"I mean we need you to take us in your wagon to Tulsa."

"Tulsa?"

"We've got no horses," Cole said.

"No horses?"

"Are you hard of hearing?" the woman asked.

He shook his head. "No ma'am." He looked around again, taking in the room. "This here is a mighty fancy place so far out in the middle of nothingness."

"Fancy?" the woman said.

"Got a right nice bar, tables, chairs, even got a privy outside and a corral and tool shed. Why you even got books on a shelf."

"We don't have time to chat about what a fancy place this is or isn't," the woman said. "We need to get to Tulsa. That man lying on the bed is dying."

"Yes'm, I could tell that by the sound of him."

"Then you will take us?" she said.

"I'm a trader, ma'am, not a teamster. I trades things."

The woman shook her head disgustedly.

"What's your offer, Mister Pepper?" Cole said.

"I remember your name, too, Mister Cole," he said. "Thing is, I'm near seventy."

"Get to the point."

"Well, I see promise in this place. I see where a man was to own this corner of the world, he might could do all right for hisself, what with it being situated at a crossroads like it is."

"You want to trade, is that it?"

He nodded. "Trade you that wagon and my mules for the whole shebang."

"Why the hell would you want it?" the woman wondered.

He looked at her with mild disapproval in his wet, brown eyes. Whether it was because he saw her as a lady who had cursed in his presence, or because she had questioned his reasoning was hard to say, but he did look at her disapprovingly. "The way I see it, a man has to take his opportunity when he sees it and this sure enough looks like opportunity to me. What's the name of this town?"

"Town?" the woman said. "This ain't no damn' town, it's just a whorehouse without whores. A saloon with nobody to drink in it. It's a damn' house of death, is what it is."

"Greasy Junction, is what they call it," Cole said.

He smiled at that, as though that suited him. "We got a deal?"

Cole looked at the woman. "Your call," he said. "I reckon you've inherited it."

"Key's above the liquor shelf," she said to George Pepper.

"Just give me time to pack my things." The two men watched as she went to the back room.

"Can I buy you a drink?" George said to Cole, then stood and went behind the bar, and looked at the bottles of liquor that hadn't already been drunk or shot to pieces.

Cole said: "You sure you don't want to just haul us into Tulsa?"

"No, suh."

"You still keep that scatter-gun under your wagon seat?"

He nodded.

"Then you better go and get it and keep it handy under the bar there," Cole said.

He looked at Cole with an understanding that comes from living and surviving a long time in a territory that held no bragging rights to longevity. "I'll do her."

"Then maybe you could help me empty out the contents of your wagon and make a pallet for my friend there to ride on?" Cole suggested.

"You ain't wantin' the goods in the back of the wagon?"

"No, sir, you keep them, maybe start yourself up a dry-goods store to go along with this whoreless whorehouse. We just need the wagon and your mules."

"I guess fortune has smiled on me."

"I wouldn't be so certain, Mister Pepper. There's four graves outside in case you've forgotten."

"Liable to be some more," he said. "But if there is, I'll be the one doing the dictating on who gets buried."

They prepared a pallet in the wagon and loaded the woman's one steamer trunk, then carried Jimmy out and placed him inside. Jimmy's badge fell out of his coat pocket as they were lifting him in. Cole picked it up, wiped a smear of blood off it, then handed it to George Pepper. "You might as well appoint yourself as law, judge, and jury like a fellow I know did down in

Texas. Might make any killing you have to do seem legal."

His dark face beamed with pleasure. "Yes, suh, I believe you right. What's a newborn town without no law." He pinned the badge to his shirt.

He was still waving as they drove off, Jimmy in the back, the woman on the seat next to Cole.

"That old man's crazy as a mud hen," she said.

"Maybe," Cole said. "Maybe not."

"Why don't you snap those reins and get these mules moving a bit faster," she said. "I'd like to get to Tulsa sooner rather than later."

"We go any faster, we'll rattle that man in the back to death."

She glanced back, brushed a sprig of hair from her forehead, then said: "I was a fool for ever leaving my home in Ohio. I had a mother and a father and three sisters. I had men who would have married me if I had let them."

The wind came out of the west, hot and stiff, and the mules walked with their heads down.

"I reckon we've all left things we sooner or later come to regret," Cole said.

"Some of us more than others."

"Don't be hard on yourself. In my book, a fool is someone who makes mistakes but won't admit it. You're no fool, Hester."

She had a wistful look in her eyes like she was remembering all the missed opportunities, the men who didn't stick around, the ones she could have married and didn't, the children she never had, her fading beauty. "I was pretty once," she said. "Damn' pretty."

"I believe you."

"Was a time when I could have had any boy in Darke County I wanted."

"Things might have turned out differently had you stayed, but that doesn't necessarily mean better."

"Ha, what would you know about it?"

"Plenty, Hester. I don't know of anyone who's lived the life they thought they ought to, do you?"

She stared straight ahead.

"I had a wife and son once," Cole said.

"You leave them somewhere behind?"

"Yes. In a grave in Missouri."

"Oh, I'm sorry to hear."

"Don't be. It was a long time ago."

"Still. . . ."

"You can have everything you want, and it can be taken from you in a heartbeat. What we do doesn't matter sometimes."

"But sometimes it does, and we end up paying for it no matter what we do the rest of our lives."

"I won't disagree with you. Just meant to say that it's not always our doing, the bad things that happen to us. What counts is what we do after the bad things have happened."

"You sound like a preacher."

"Far from it."

They stopped by a stream and helped Jimmy out of the back of the wagon. Cole walked him down to some bushes while Hester fixed them a lunch of canned meat she sliced onto crackers. She spread a blanket on the ground and produced a bottle of red wine she'd taken from Mr. St. John's saloon, and if one didn't think too hard about the situation, they might have been just three friends out for a picnic, sitting there by that little stream, eating meat and cracker sandwiches, and drinking wine on a blue blanket.

The sun stood straight up and was warm on their faces. After they ate, Jimmy said he was tired and wouldn't mind if he slept for a half hour there on the blanket with the sun warm on him. Hester said she wanted to go downstream and bathe in the creek. Cole sat, cross-legged, and smoked a cigarette and tried not to think too hard about Anna Wild Bird, her dying husband there on the blanket, or the woman bathing in the creek. It wasn't easy to do.

Later, Hester came up from the creek, drying her hair that she'd unpinned and that now hung in wet tangles to her shoulders. She looked scrubbed clean and was wearing the fresh clothes she'd taken from her trunk; she carried the old clothes in a bundle under her arm.

"I feel renewed," she said. Her cheeks were rosy.

"The power of water," Cole said.

"What?"

"They say that water has the power to renew you."

"Oh. Are you sure you never preached before? You sound like a sin-and-redemption man . . . a fellow who would stand out in the river baptizing and waiting for the Holy Spirit to descend down like a dove."

"You seem to know a good deal about it."

"I was baptized in the Ohio River by a preacher who later took my virginity. Yes, I know a thing or two about water ritual and holy words and sinful deeds, Mister Cole." She sat down on the blanket and drank some of the wine. "You never was tempted to marry again?" she asked.

"No."

She looked at him with a haunting stare. "You're not a bad-looking man."

He rubbed the stubble on his chin. "That wine's gone to your head. I must look like a slag heap."

"A little rough, but I've seen worse."

"Best we wake Jimmy and get back on the road to Tulsa."

She took another sip of wine from the bottle, looked at Cole over the top of it. "Thank you," she said.

"For what?"

"For being a kind and decent man. I've not met many along the way."

"I should be the one thanking you."

"My turn to ask . . . for what?" she said.

"For all the help you've been to us."

Cole awakened Jimmy and assisted him into the wagon, then climbed up on the seat next to Hester. She had her face tilted toward the sun, a slight smile curving her lips. "It's turned into a nice day," she said. "At least I don't see any crows, do you?"

CHAPTER TWENTY-TWO

A voice called to Anna in the night, but when she went to the door, no one was there. Moonlight lay in the yard like a thin silver blanket, and a rush of wind flowed through the trees and caused their leaves to quake. Had she been dreaming? Was it the voice of Jimmy calling to her? Perhaps. But the voice sounded as though it came from beyond the grave, for it was unearthly and the voice said only this: *I flow from you like a river flows from the great water and empties into nothingness. I am the lost child, the forever being of your blood.*

This she did not understand but something seemed to etch itself in her bones and the feeling edified in her blood until she felt a vibrancy she'd only felt once before and it caused her to remember the child they had taken from her at birth. Secretly, in her heart, she had called the boy Thomas. But it was all she had to connect her to the infant, a single name she kept locked in her heart like a precious stone or a pretty shell locked in a tin box. For that is what her heart felt like afterward—a tin box with naught but the smallest treasure.

"Thomas," she said to the gusting wind that rattled out of the trees and across the yard, blowing before it loose leaves that did a tumbling dance in the pewter light. "Thomas . . . ." But no one answered, and her heart beat faintly against her breast. Faint and quivering and longing. There was only wind and moonlight and darkness, the thump, thump of her heart, and the madness that lies embedded in loss.

She went back inside and lit a lamp and turned up the wick until the room filled with warm yellow light. She stoked the fire she kept burning in the stove and set a pot of coffee on to brew. She paced the room and looked out the window and went to the door again and looked out and saw only pale light.

She could feel the child there between her legs, the weight of it bearing on her, struggling to be free of her womb—the hands of Rudina helping it from her. The light played on Rudina's face, her brow glistening with sweat as she bent to the task of birthing the child, speaking cautionary words of encouragement. She remembered the rain that night, how it drummed against the roof and drove itself against the windows, a cold October rain that had in it a certain dark sorrow, as if foretelling the child's future, the shame that would accompany both of them, woman and child, mother and son. She had laid tortured on the bed, never crying out as Rudina labored to bring the infant forth and the smoldering in her loins was like fire—a consuming blaze of heat that would forever mark them—mother and son.

She sat now at the table, the tin cup of bitter dark coffee warming between her hands and tried not to remember it— when her father came and took the child and later, when she had awakened to a gray light, the air cool and heavy after the all-night rain, the sound of thunder still reminiscent in her dreams. Her arms were empty, the bundle of bloody swaddling clothes near a metal pan of pink-tinged water. But remember she did. The room was empty and frail. Only Rudina was there, dozing in a chair by her bed, coming awake when she asked about the child.

"He has taken him," was all Rudina had said, her own eyes full of empty weariness.

And later when her father had entered the room, his face dark and twisted as a mesquite stump, he had said: "It is finished. The child is dead. This will be forgotten and there will be no talk of this from now on." Then he had turned and walked out again.

She sipped the coffee and tried not to hear those harsh and terrible words, tried not to think of the infant in that season of her regret. It had all been so long ago that she was barely sure that the event had actually occurred—it was like a dream within a dream. It was like something she had made up or had wished for—a little girl's dreams of bearing the child of her lover—but in truth she knew the reality. And all these years she'd believed that the child had died, but the wind this night had come and told a different story and it troubled her greatly.

Her father had sent her away to a boarding school in Pennsylvania where she'd learned Latin and guard against her posture and other things that stole her spirit as she lay in a small room each night until the loneliness of it felt like the weight of rocks on her chest. This lasted until her father considered she had learned enough about propriety and other matters of the heart, until she had forgotten the white man. Her exile lasted until she had forgotten the issue of blood and quivering flesh and the single cry as the infant took its first breath, then was taken from her.

The night wind sang as she drank her coffee, and twice more she thought she heard her name being called. But when she went to the door, no one was there. Thus she stayed until dawn, sitting at the table, drinking coffee and trying to make sense of it all.

Maybe, she thought as the morning crept through the window, *I should have said something to him. Maybe I should have told him there was a child who was born of night and blood . . . whose shame and sin were not his own. Whose fate was little known beyond the lies her father had spoken* "Thomas," she said as she rested her face in her hands. "Thomas. . . ."

Chapter Twenty-Three

John Henry Cole, Hester Price, and Jimmy Wild Bird arrived in Tulsa late the second day, under a blood-red sun that reflected itself in the windows along the east side of the street. Hester said that she remembered the town's best doctor kept an office above a harness shop and so it was there they went first.

Climbing the outside stairs, Cole saw a note tacked on the door that read: *Out On Errand, Be Back Soon!* He delivered the news to Hester and asked if she knew of any other doctors. She said there was a man given to the practice of medicine on horses and whores (the medico out on the errand, she said, was a pious man who would not treat whores or syphilitic cowboys) and that his name was Clarence Bellringer.

"Where would we find him?" Cole asked.

"Well, if he's not yet dead from alcohol, or the bullet of a jealous husband, we'd most likely find him at Huang Yü's opium den . . . Clarence is a dope fiend, among other things."

"Great, I'm sure Jimmy Wild Bird will be happy to learn he's about to be treated by a dope-fiend horse doctor," Cole said. "Point the way."

There was a small Chinese section on Tulsa's outskirts and they drove there and stopped in front of a false-fronted building that had ducks hanging by their feet in the window.

"I'll go in with you," Hester said. "Huang Yü knows me."

"No need," Cole said.

"There is unless you speak Mandarin," she said.

"You do?"

She nodded. "Enough to make myself understood."

"You continue to surprise me, Hester."

"You had your chance yesterday, cowboy. An offer like me only comes along once." Her wink was sly, tinged with devilment. It was good to see her smile.

The Celestial stood behind the counter waiting on a woman who looked to be as ancient as the Old Testament. They spoke in rapid-fire lingo and finally the Celestial wrapped a duck in butcher paper and gave it to the woman and she left without looking at either Hester or Cole directly.

Hester spoke to the Chinaman, and he nodded and smiled like she'd just told him his cousins had all arrived from the Orient with their pockets full of gold. Then he led them down a trap door to an underground room that was pungent and dim. Smoke drifted in and out of the flames of lit candles. Lying on pallets were men in various states of stupor. The old man led them to a solitary individual, lying in a corner on a straw mat, his face turned to the wall. The Celestial kneeled and spoke to the man on the pallet in broken English. The man turned over and looked at the visitors through the haze of opium smoke.

"Eh?"

"Clarence, it's me, Hester."

He shook his head as if he didn't understand. The Celestial held the light up close to her face. "Oh, it's you, Hester. . . ."

"We need your help, Clarence. We got a man that's been shot and probably will die if someone don't help him quick."

The man eased himself to a sitting position, leaned on one elbow, and looked at John Henry Cole.

"Who's this?"

She told him.

"Oh," he said.

They helped him up and to climb the stairs and finally to

step out into the twilight.

"Glorious," the man said as he stood there, looking around, patting his pockets as though he were looking for something he'd lost.

"What's glorious?" Hester asked.

"Damned if I know. Where's the patient?"

They showed him Jimmy in the back of the wagon.

"Bring him to my place," Clarence said. "Follow me."

"You want to ride, Clarence?" Hester said. "You look un-stable."

"Hell, I *am* unstable, child. Was I to climb up in that wagon and fall out, I'd surely bust my neck. Follow me."

They did, down to a fine brick home that sat at the very edge of town between the town proper and the Chinese district. Cole looked at Hester as he hauled back on the reins. She said: "Clarence's daddy was a big-time doctor back East in case you're wondering."

They took Jimmy inside and Clarence led them to a room that had a table for the patient to lie on and a cabinet full of surgical instruments and whiskey bottles filled to various levels. Clarence washed his hands and face in a pan of water, then dried them with a towel and asked Cole to hold one of the oil lamps close to the patient so he could see the damage. Cole did.

Clarence examined Jimmy's arm, then the flesh wound in his side, and straightened and shook his head. "Arm's gonna have to come off."

Jimmy looked at him, shook his head. "No it ain't."

"Then you will die a not too pleasant death," Clarence said.

"I'm not going to let you take my arm off."

"Suit yourself." Clarence turned his back on Jimmy and said generally: "Anybody up for a drink?"

Without waiting for a vote, he went to the medicine cabinet, selected one of the bottles, and began filling drinking glasses. When he finished, he handed one each to Hester and Cole. "Raise him up so he can drink," he said.

Cole raised Jimmy up.

Jimmy said: "I'm not a drinking man."

"You will be by the time this is all over," Clarence said. "You folks et?"

Hester said they hadn't and Clarence left the room and in a moment they could hear a bell being rung followed by conversation that sounded like it was in Mandarin, then Clarence reëntered the room and said: "My girl will fix us some supper."

"What about him?" Cole said, nodding toward Jimmy.

"You heard the man. He don't want to lose his arm. I respect a man's wishes. It's his choice."

"It's a damned foolish choice," Hester said.

"I'd like it if you was to remove me from this hard table," Jimmy said. "I don't mind dying so much, but not lying on a table like a side of beef."

They helped him into one of the guest rooms that Clarence showed them. It was a fancy room with a Brussels carpet, a four-poster bed, wine-red velvet drapes, and three or four paintings of young girls in white dresses with dogs curled at their feet. The girls all had smiles and so did the dogs.

"He can die in here," Clarence said. "He wouldn't be the first."

"Good God, Clarence, do you have to be so morbid?" Hester hissed.

"Dying's just one more transition in this travail we call life, nothing to get so worked up over, Hester. He knows he's going to die if he keeps that arm, and we know it, no sense pussyfooting around the issue."

She shook her head and said: "Leave me alone with him to get him settled."

Clarence and Cole went out to a large room with a polished table that looked like it could seat Custer's army and he said: "Take any seat you want, we won't be having extra guests join us tonight."

"Do you ever?"

"No. Seegar?" He went to a teakwood sideboard that had figures carved into the legs and took from it a box of cigars and offered Cole one. Then he poured them another drink, and sat at the head of the table and dipped the end of his cigar in his liquor before putting it in his mouth. "Brandy and cigars," he said. "Just one of my weaknesses. I have several."

"Being poor isn't one of them," Cole said, looking around the room. There was a fireplace along one wall that could have housed a family of homesteaders.

"A curse, to be sure," he said, blowing circles of smoke.

"How is it a curse to be rich?"

"When a man has much, little is required of him. My family has always had much and has always given me much. As a result, Mister Cole, not much has ever been required of me. Thus it was I quit medical school and came West as an adventure. It is here where I was seduced by dope and harlots, and here where I chose to stay. The greater the depravity, the greater the attraction. Such pursuits don't leave much time for accomplishments of a higher order. My father would have had me become a bona-fide physician like himself. I fell far short of his goals for me. So you see, in my case, wealth has been a sort of curse."

"I know a lot of men who wouldn't mind being cursed if this is what it means."

"Would you be among them?"

"I'd have to think about it some."

"An honest answer," he said, drawing deeply on the cigar before exhaling a ring of gray smoke.

"Can I ask if your father is so disappointed in you, why has he given you all this?"

"As a reminder that he is still the father, and I the needful son. For you see, Mister Cole, even unmitigated failure does not sever the blood ties. I am his shame, his burden, his cross to bear, and he bears it well. Without me, his charitable work would be diminished by half. So you see, in a rather perverse way, everyone benefits. We all, in the end, get what we want. And we all know to be careful of what we want, for we just may get it. More brandy?"

Hester entered the room and said that Jimmy wanted to talk to Cole privately.

"I'm not going to make it," Jimmy said when Cole entered the room and pulled up a chair.

"You would, if you'd let that man take off your arm."

"I won't," he said. "I'd just as soon be dead as to be half a man."

"Knew lots of men who lost an arm or a leg in the war," Cole said. "It didn't make any of them half of what they were."

"You don't understand."

"I understand you'll take your damned pride to the grave with you."

He looked shrunken there in the bed, his features wan. Cole could see the fight had gone out of him, the eyes resigned to whatever awaited him beyond this life. "I want you to go back and tell Anna. . . ."

"Tell her what?"

"That I died."

"That's something I don't want you to put on me."

"Why not? Seems only right she should hear it from you."

"What's that supposed to mean?"

"I know about you and Anna. I've known for a long time. Her daddy told me before I married her that she loved a white man . . . a deputy marshal from Fort Smith. He even told me your name."

"That was a long time back," Cole said. "There's nothing between us now."

"You don't need to shake my tree, John Henry. I saw the way you two looked at each other the day you and Digger rode up."

"You're wrong."

"Tell me I'm wrong that she called your name in her sleep the night before we left."

"Look, Jimmy. . . ."

He shook his head sharply to cut Cole off. "I'm not up to god-damn' debating it."

"I'm not going back to tell your wife you died because of your god-damned pride. Get somebody else."

"Why'd you come in the first place?"

"Because Parker asked me to."

"Bullshit!"

"Think what you want."

"You came because you found out it had something to do with Anna."

Cole strung his fingers through his hair, wishing he was any place but sitting in that room with the husband of the woman he loved.

"I ain't jealous no more," Jimmy said. "I was for a long time. Anna and me are of the same blood . . . Indian blood. You're a white man . . . what you expect me to feel?"

"What's color got to do with it?"

"Everything. Nothing. . . ."

"What the hell you want from me . . . to say I'm sorry for loving her before you came along?"

His face was knotted in pain that came from more than just his wounds. "Just go back and tell her I loved her and I'm sorry I couldn't love her as much as she needed."

"It's not my place to say such things," Cole said. He looked toward the heavy drapes, the fancy wallpaper, his eyes flinching.

"Did you know she had a child?"

Cole's temples began to throb.

"Not our child, but one she had before I married her."

"What are you trying to tell me?"

"She was only with one other man before she met me, far as I know. . . ."

Cole could feel the heat of revelation racing through his blood like bad whiskey. "No, that's not possible."

"Why not? Are you saying that you were never with her?"

The memory of their intimacy that last day in the hotel flashed in Cole's mind like a tintype reflecting the sun.

"The child was yours, John Henry Cole."

Cole shook his head. "You're lying."

Jimmy nodded, bringing his reddened gaze around to rest on Cole. "Why would I lie about a god-damn' thing like that? About a thing that brought her untold shame and heartbreak? About a thing that she would never speak of with me, her god-damn' husband? Tell me why I'd lie about something like that, John Henry?"

Cole felt a knife of pain stab deep enough to pierce his soul. "Tell me about it," he said.

Jimmy told Cole the story of how the very night the baby was born, Anna's father, the man who hated Cole so terribly because of the color of his skin and his station in life as a paid man-hunter, had come and taken the child away. Jimmy said that the old man never would reveal what he did with it, but he told Anna that the baby had died. "I heard later it wasn't true . . . that the baby hadn't died. . . ."

Cole could hear his blood banging in his ears.

"That old man was a son-of-a-bitch for what he done to Anna. And maybe I been a son-of-a-bitch, too, for not telling her what I heard later on. Her old man got god-damn' good and drunk one day and fell from a wagon, and the wheels rolled over his neck and killed him, and it was a fitting death. Now my turn's come around, but I ain't going to go to the grave carrying this secret. . . ."

"How do you know the rumor is true, that the baby didn't die, that maybe the old man didn't take it out and smother it?"

Jimmy shook his head. "I don't know for sure, and I never really wanted to find out. I didn't want it to get between Anna and me. . . ." He gasped and something visible shivered through him. "I figured, all that time gone by, it could only bring her more heartache to find out maybe the child was still alive. . . ."

Cole was angry and hurt and feeling as helpless as he ever had. He wondered why Anna had never told him that she was pregnant, but then he remembered that after he'd left the Nations, he was on the drift for a long time and there was no way she could have told him—except for when he had returned, that afternoon, there in the house when they'd almost made love. She could have told him then, but she didn't.

Jimmy coughed, cleared his throat. "What I heard was, the old man gave that child to the woman he used to carry on with . . . she was his housekeeper. I heard the woman took the baby and went away. . . ."

"Where?"

"I don't know. I never pursued it. Didn't want to pursue it. Now, if you don't mind, get the hell out of here and leave me to settle the rest of my affairs. Ask Hester to come in and bring me a pencil and some paper. I want to write out my will."

Jimmy looked away toward the wall. His conversation with Cole was over.

Cole walked out and told Hester what Jimmy wanted, then went out onto the gallery, and stood there in the cool night air and took in deep breaths and tried to get his thoughts in order. The news of the child rippled through his blood like an undercurrent so deep it felt like he was drowning in it. He walked back in the house, down the hall, and into the room where Hester was sitting next to Jimmy's bed, writing down his words on a ledger.

"Just one question," Cole said.

Jimmy looked up, his eyes cold as a dead man's. "It was a boy," he said.

Later Clarence found John Henry Cole drunk in the yard.

"We could go to Huang Yü's dope den, if you really want to forget whatever your problems are, Mister Cole."

"Nothing's going to make me forget what I know, Doc."

"I understand perfectly," he said. "I've been trying for years to erase the memory of my existence and nothing's worked so far. But when I'm at Huang Yü's, I come mighty close to a blue heaven where nothing really much matters. Not even the truth of what sad and pitiful creatures we've become."

"You see, Doc, I don't want to forget. The truth is my burden and I have to carry it."

"Why you poor miserable son-of-a-bitch. I guess we all got our crosses to carry. My dear old daddy, me, you, that stubborn Indian, Hester . . . every last one of us." He stood there, looking up at the first star of the night. "It's like He's watching us. Like He's watching to see what sort of mayhem and misery we'll cause each other next. Has He forgotten that he made us in His own image and, if we are craven idols, then so is He!"

"Leave me alone, Doc. Go in there and sit with Jimmy Wild Bird and preach over him and offer him your dope and pull the sheet o'er him when he's gone. Then come and tell me about it."

"You're a hard man, Cole."

But the hardness Clarence perceived in Cole had been shattered like glass against stone by the revelation of the child, and Cole could do little more than try and drink away his miserable heart and call silently to the woman who had suffered for the two of them. He had promised Anna he would help Jimmy, and now Jimmy was as good as dead, and it seemed to Cole, and maybe it would seem to Anna, too, that Cole had let him die. Cole would have to go back and tell her that he'd failed, and she'd have always to wonder about Cole, and Cole would have always to wonder about himself. Yes, with Jimmy dead, Anna was free, but that's not the way Cole wanted it. Still, with the turn of events, knowing Anna had had Cole's child—Cole wasn't sure he was sorry Jimmy was out of the way. Cole cursed his fall from grace while the storm of confusion, shame, and anger grew in his mind. He drank until the blackness took him.

CHAPTER TWENTY-FOUR

In three days' time, only two cowboys came, a pair of waddies from some far-flung ranch. One was off-eyed and the other runty, and they rode gaunt horses and had shaggy mustaches.

"Where's Mister Saint John?" one said.

"Where's the whores?" the other said.

"Gone," George said.

"Gone?" the cowboys said in unison.

"Yes, sir."

"We rode near forty miles to have a go at them whores, and drink ourselves silly," the off-eyed cowboy said.

"Forty god-damn' long dusty miles," the runty one said.

"I got whiskey, but the whores is gone," George Pepper said.

"Shit," they said, again in unison.

"You still want to drink yourselves silly?" George asked.

"Might just as well," the off-eyed one said.

"Might just as god-damn' well," the runty one said.

They were both mighty sore there were no whores for them to visit and discussed it at length as they drank.

"I got half a month's wages I was going to spend on that flaxen-haired whore," Off-Eye said.

"And I was going to spend mine on the other," Runty said.

George made sure he kept their glasses full and wiped the bar as they drank.

"Saint John light out, or what?" Off-Eye asked.

"Way I got the story," George said, "he got shot through the brains."

"Shot through the brains?"

"Who shot him?" said Runty.

"Some renegades."

The cowboys shook their heads sympathetically.

"It's a god-damn' wild land, this here is," Off-Eye said.

"Shot one of the whores, too," George said.

"Shot one of the whores?" Runty said. "Which one did they shoot?"

"I don't know, I wasn't here."

"God, I hope it wasn't the flaxen-haired one," Off-Eye said.

George poured them more whiskey and offered them each cigars to go along with their whiskey. "Drink up," he said. "I got plenty of liquor."

"You ought to get a piano," Runty said. "A piano and some whores is what this place could stand."

George told them he would consider it.

The two cowboys drank until it got to be midnight and beyond, then they laid down in a corner and slept until morning, then got up and rode off. George realized, if he was to have a going concern, he would have to hire a whore or two, lest word get out among the cowboys that there were no whores left at Greasy Junction. He determined that as soon as somebody came through with a wagon, he would catch a ride into Tulsa and set about hiring one or two whores and maybe see if somebody had a piano to sell. Nobody knew what would make a cowboy happy except a cowboy; they were an odd and craven lot and could be mean and shoot all the windows out of a saloon and kill the bartender. George felt lucky that the two cowboys hadn't turned mean in their drinking. Still, he sort of wished now that he had his mules and wagon back. Being a business owner and mayor didn't seem all it was cracked up to be. What good was being the mayor of a place that in three days' time only saw two down-at-the-heels, complaining cowboys. George toted up his profits and it came to $7.10.

Two days after the cowboys left, four more riders came. Three Indians and one white man. George knew who they were the minute he laid eyes on them. But they had caught him unawares, for he was just coming from the privy with an issue of the *Police Gazette* in his hands and his thoughts elsewhere when the four rode up.

They sat their horses and looked him over good and the white man spoke: "Say there, nigger, you got any customers inside what got bullet holes in them?"

George shook his head. "What this look like, a horsepital?" He was trying to put a little humor into it, for they looked like mighty desperate men.

The white man stood in his stirrups and looked around at the others and said: "Looks like we got us a nigger that thinks we're foolin' around here."

One of the Indians, a rank-looking boy, took out his pistol and shot George in the foot and said: "You better get to telling us about them god-damn' sons-a-bitches pretty quick, you old fool, or I'll shoot your feet, and then shoot out your god-damn' eyes!"

The white man took his lariat, undid it, and made a loop, then swung it over his head and tossed it so the loop landed over George. Then he pulled the rope up short and the loop tightened around George Pepper's ankles. "You want me to drag you off through the scrub?"

George Pepper had little choice but to tell them what they wanted to know, that the two men and the woman had taken his wagon and gone to Tulsa. When the Indian that had shot him asked what kind of wagon it was, he told him it was a big blue wagon with his name painted on the sides and the Indian said—"Shit."—and shot him through the chest.

The boy saw the black man stumble backward from the bullet, stagger, and fall, clutching his chest as though to catch the blood. He saw him rise again and stumble on toward the dugout and reach the door and stumble inside, falling as he did. They followed the old man inside and saw him lying there on his back, his arms flung outward, his eyes half open. As the man lay there, his eyes shifted and came to rest on the boy's. Red Snake saw the peaceful wonderment in the old man's eyes and envied him his dying.

I know, old man, he said silently, the words flowing from his heart to that of the old man. *I know you have gone to that place where the water is sweet and the sky is always blue and antelope are as plentiful as grass. I will go there, too, very soon.*

Billy Starr walked up and kicked the old man once to see if he was still alive, and when he was satisfied that he wasn't, they began to drink the whiskey until their minds were wild with it. Then when they were plenty drunk, Caddo held aloft his empty bottle and said—"Let's get our asses in the wind."—and they rode off toward Tulsa, their hearts full of murder.

CHAPTER TWENTY-FIVE

They formed a deathwatch—Clarence, Hester, and John Henry Cole. Jimmy Wild Bird's words about the child were still tearing at Cole's consciousness like jagged glass against silk.

"The poison's all through him," Clarence said on the fourth day. "It won't be long now."

"Can't you do something?" Hester asked. "He's out of his mind with fever. Couldn't you chloroform him and cut off his arm?"

"Too late for that," Clarence said.

"How long's he got?" Cole asked.

Clarence shrugged. "Day, maybe two, maybe not even that."

They waited, mostly in silence. That evening of the fourth day, Clarence said he was going to the Chinese section. If the Indian died before he got back, there was an undertaker in town who would come and take the body.

Cole and Hester sat in the evening air on the gallery, listening to the cicadas. The buzz of the insects seemed like the frenetic cry of lost souls rising from their graves, gathering off in the woods, waiting, waiting, for Jimmy Wild Bird's spirit to pass among them.

"Seems a shame a man so young has to die out of stubbornness and vanity," Hester said. She was drinking peach brandy.

Cole was drinking whiskey and branch water. "A man needs to hold onto something in this world. Pride's as good as anything, I reckon."

"Pride is stubbornness," she said. "The worst kind, and it's killing him."

"What can I say, Hester? Every man has a right to live and die the way he chooses."

"Men are such god-damned fools," she said.

"You'll get no argument from me."

"I can't wait to clear out, go back East," she said. The brandy seemed to glow like liquid sun in her glass.

"Heading back to Darke County?"

"I've come to learn there are a lot of worse places than Darke County." She had a faraway look in her eyes when she said it.

"Maybe settle down, marry a local boy, have some kids?"

She held the glass like a chalice cup and stared into it. "You think I'm foolish, having such thoughts?"

"No. I don't think you're foolish. Who doesn't want to be happy and at peace?"

She sipped some more of the brandy thoughtfully, then said: "Yes, but who would want to marry a whore, right?"

"Who has to know about your past unless you tell them?"

"I'd not want to deceive a man who was willing to marry me."

"We've all done things we're not proud of, Hester. Doesn't mean we're not good people because we did those things. A man who loves you true enough, it won't matter to him what you done before he came along."

She shook her head and smiled, her teeth white in the dying plum-colored light. "I'd like to be the woman who has your heart. You're a good man, John Henry."

There was something in her words that caused the ache to stir in Cole again. "Not as good as I would like, Hester."

"Like you said, we've all done things we're not proud of. Doesn't make you a bad man any more than whoring makes me a bad woman. Ain't that what you just said?"

Cole told her what Jimmy had revealed about the child. She listened with her eyes closed and didn't say anything for a time, then opened her eyes and looked at him and said: "So you don't know if he's alive or dead?"

Cole shook his head. "No."

"How sad for both of you."

Cole rolled each of them a cigarette and they sat there, smoking. "I don't know why I told you," he said after a long silence.

"Because you had to tell someone who wouldn't pass judgment on you and you knew that I wouldn't."

"Maybe that's it."

"Confession's good for the soul."

"Where'd you hear that?"

"That's what that preacher who baptized me and took my virginity told me just before he did both those things."

"You confessed to him."

"Yes, my adoration for him, my weakness for him, my need of him and for salvation."

"Then maybe confession isn't such a good thing, after all."

"Depends on who you confess to," she said. "He was a fellow more interested in bloomers than Bibles. They ain't all that way, I hope. You're not that way."

"You're not planning on dunking me in the river, are you, Hester?"

She laughed, and her laughter was a good thing to hear and helped ease some of the somber mood of their situations. "I guess we could beat ourselves to death with our misgivings," Cole said.

She sighed. "That poor man in there. . . ."

"I know."

It was morning before Clarence returned. When he saw them sitting on the gallery, Hester's eyes rimmed red, he knew. "He dead?"

"Earlier this morning," Cole said.

"Well, at least he's out from under his load of suffering. You want, I'll go and get the undertaker, save you the trouble."

"No," Cole said. "I'll do it. I owe him that much."

Cole arranged for Jimmy Wild Bird's burial, knowing that when the task was completed, he had to go back and see Anna and tell her and ask about the child. He knew it wasn't finished between them, just as the business at hand wasn't finished. But for now, rounding up the renegades would have to wait.

It rained later that morning, and they stood there next to the grave site, just the three of them and the undertaker and a half-breed who'd dug the grave. The undertaker spoke a few words about the brevity of life and dying and meeting Jesus and returning to dust. The rain beat down on the coffin, and Hester dropped in some wildflowers she'd collected just before it rained, and they lay like stick figures with red and blue heads on the wet wood. Clarence pulled a silver flask from his coat pocket while the undertaker was still talking about "a man's eternal soul" and took a pull and handed it to Cole. Cole took a pull, and handed it to Hester.

"Do you think he would approve of us drinking over his grave?" she asked.

"I don't think he'd be offended," Clarence said.

She took a pull and handed back the bottle, and Clarence leaned over the grave and spilled some of his whiskey in, saying: "Maybe it will help keep you warm on your journey."

They walked through the rain back toward the large brick house. Cole told them of his plans to return to Talaquah and tell Anna the news. Hester said: "Do you mind if I ride that far with you, since I'm going East myself."

Cole told her he didn't mind, and Clarence took a fancy metal box from a shelf and from it took cash money and handed it to her, saying: "For a new start in life."

She thanked him and said she couldn't take it, and he said she ought to because he had lots of it coming in every month and all he was bound to do was to smoke it up at Huang Yü's dope house and give it to Chinese whores, and she might just as well have it as the dope and the whores. She kissed him on the cheek, and he might have blushed, or it could have simply been the whiskey in his blood that turned his cheeks florid. He made them the offer of a buggy and a horse, and when Cole explained that he couldn't afford the rig, he said he'd take the big blue wagon and team of mules in exchange. Cole said it was a generous offer but hardly a fair trade for him.

"Why, I'd look all the rage driving around town in it," he said jovially.

They shook hands all around and left that very afternoon. After an hour of silence Hester said: "Your eyes are full of trouble."

"It's not over."

"What's not?"

"None of it."

"You did what you could."

"It wasn't enough, Hester. It wasn't nearly enough." In the east, they saw the dark denim sky split like a torn seam allowing the thinnest blade of sunlight to penetrate and glow along the road until it looked gold-paved. And there in a distant field, where half-grown corn stood dark green, the ground was covered with crows.

CHAPTER TWENTY-SIX

Pablo saw the crows—a dark ring of black against a denim sky, the color of which reminded him of his dead wife's eyes. The wind shifted from west to east as he topped a rise and saw the cabin below and the scent of death, caught on the wind, drifted up and caused his nostrils to flare. The horse stamped the ground and shifted its hind legs because it, too, smelled the same death. Pablo took the rifle from its boot and laid it across the pommel of his saddle and urged the horse down the slope toward the cabin.

He didn't see any horses where horses should be. The corral was empty. All he saw were the crows circling, dropping to earth, rising up again at his approach, their caws fierce against the stillness.

The door to the privy stood open and Pablo could see it had been shot full of holes. He could see, too, that the glass had been shot out of the cabin's windows and he could see the four depressions in the earth near the cabin that indicated freshly dug graves.

"Bad place," he said to the horse.

The door to the cabin stood ajar. He dismounted, holding the rifle at the ready, and went in. It took a moment or two for his vision to adjust to the dim light, but it didn't take any time at all to smell the fetid odor of death there in the room. He saw books—some of them torn and lying open on the floor, and others standing on shelves. He saw blood—a long trail of reddish brown from behind the bar that would forever stain the floorboards. He saw a bed in the corner and busted whiskey bottles atop the bar and motes of dust in the light coming through the broken windows. He saw two feet angling outward, toes pointing toward the ceiling.

The rifle felt hot in his hands. He looked around the corner of the bar. The dead man was bloated, but Pablo recognized the man. He looked, then backed away. The man's shirt front was blood-soaked and crawling with maggots.

He stepped outside the cabin and took in a deep breath of air and leaned against the cabin's wall where the sunlight struck it and felt the warmth through his shirt because just then his blood felt cold and distant to him—more distant than the sun. He knew in his heart who had done this thing. He walked about reading sign around the cabin, saw a dropped button from a waistcoat—a silver concho (the same one he'd seen the white renegade wearing sewn to his trousers that fateful day) and that confirmed it had been the renegades. The tracks led off toward the northwest.

He didn't feel up to digging any graves, though he felt mighty terrible about the death of the black man. It was another case, he thought to himself, of kindness being repaid with unkindness, and he looked up at the sky, the circle of crows, and wondered if maybe God had been asleep.

"He has to be sleeping," he said to the horse as he stroked its wet black nostrils. "Only a God who was sleeping would allow such things to happen."

He found a can of kerosene in a shed near the corral and spilled the contents inside the cabin, then struck a match and dropped it to the wetness and immediately the flames flared and the fire traced through the cabin in a snaky orange line. He went outside again, taking a bottle of whiskey with him, and led the horse over to the water trough, let it drink, and watched as the flames consumed the cabin, knowing he'd done the only thing he could for the man inside. *Like hell,* he thought as the fire quickly burned through the walls and roof of the cabin. *This is what hell must be like, hot and full of uncontrollable force.* But then he wondered, too, if a man was already dead when he went to hell, how would he be made to suffer the lake of fire his wife had often spoken of after she'd been taught the white man's religion. This thought troubled him as he sat and ate what little lunch he had—a few crackers and some of the whiskey—and watched the cabin collapse in on itself with a great woosh!

"*Aii,* so much death," he said to the horse in whose dark eyes the flames were reflected. "When will it stop, eh?"

The horse pawed the ground and snorted, and pretty soon Pablo mounted, securing the whiskey bottle, and turned it away from the dying embers and headed it in a line with the faded hoof prints of the renegade riders. He rode until the sky turned plum, its edges flaring black silver, and the moon rose above the trees, fat and white as a blinded eye. He reined in at the edge of some woods and removed his saddle and blanket, then slept, his head full of dreams. None of them good. And in his dreams, he heard the cawing of crows and felt the dusting of their wings upon his face.

CHAPTER TWENTY-SEVEN

It took three days for John Henry Cole and Hester Price to arrive at Talaquah. Bone Blue was sitting outside his office with a black and white dog resting at his feet. Cole saw the look in his eyes when they pulled up in the buggy.

He looked back up the road leading into town, didn't see Jimmy Wild Bird, and Cole opined that he already knew why. "You had trouble?"

"More than we could handle," Cole said. "This is Hester Price." He helped her down, and she looked at Bone, at the badge he wore openly on his coat lapel.

"You look used up, ma'am," Bone said. "You-all want to step inside?"

They went in. It was a spare room, a gun rack along one wall, a small, scarred desk with a ladder-back chair, a spittoon, a checkerboard, dust along the windowsills.

Bone offered Hester the chair. "Where's Jimmy at?" he asked.

"He died of gangrene from a bullet wound to the arm," Cole stated.

"A bullet wound to the arm?"

"He wouldn't let a doctor cut off his arm."

"Damn. . . ." Bone looked off toward the window, the metallic light spreading out across his desk, the floor, Hester sitting on the chair. "You want to fill me in on the details?" Bone said after a moment.

Cole told him the story and watched his face knot into pain.

"Those god-damn' sons-a-bitches," he said. Then looked at Hester and said: "Pardon, ma'am."

She waved off the apology. "I'd like a place to get a hot bath and a fresh change of clothes," she said.

Bone nodded. "Down the street is a hotel where you can get a room and a hot bath."

"Thanks." She stood and said to Cole: "I'll see you later, then?"

"I've got some business I need to take care of," he said. "I'm not sure how long it will take, but I'll drop by and check on you when I'm finished."

They watched her leave, then Bone pulled a bottle of Mexican liquor from the bottom drawer of the desk and jerked the cork from it before tipping it back and taking a hard hit. He handed it to Cole who declined. His gaze was narrow, doubtful. "Jimmy was my best friend, John Henry."

"I know."

"And you didn't kill any of them sons-a-bitches?"

"Killed one, the rest got in the wind."

"One," he repeated, as though trying to calculate the number in his head. One didn't seem to fit into anything, didn't seem to equal the loss. "One. God damn! One ain't shit."

"I've got business to take care of," Cole said. "I'll catch you later."

He took another hit of the liquor. "You think it's your duty to ride out and tell Anna?"

"I was there," Cole said. "Jimmy gave me a message for her. I intend to deliver it."

He started to turn when Bone called his name like a curse. "Cole!"

"Don't make this difficult," Cole said. "I'm in a bad mood."

Bone held the liquor bottle in one hand down alongside his leg, held it by the neck in a way that was easy enough to swing

189

if he wanted to. But he didn't want to.

"Whatever you're thinking went on out there," Cole said, "I told you the truth of it. I didn't let him die."

"You and Anna . . . ," he started to say.

"Let it be, Bone."

"I know it all. Jimmy told me about it."

"You're mad and hurt because you lost your best friend. I'll take that into account, but you let off with any talk about Anna and me."

"Go on, then, god damn it! Get the hell out of my office!"

Anna was standing in light when Cole rode up. The sun fell on her with a grace that made her seem radiant and pure. She stood there as if she'd been waiting for him and she didn't move until he had dismounted from the buggy and walked up to her.

"You've brought me news of Jimmy, haven't you?"

Cole nodded.

"I had dreams about it after you left. I saw him lying in a coffin, his hair combed all wrong. I saw you, too, same way, your hair combed all wrong . . . through a glass in the lid."

Cole remembered thinking when he had seen the way the undertaker had prepared Jimmy that it didn't look like him. He knew now it was the way his hair was combed. He explained to her what had happened. She flinched in the telling.

"It's anybody's guess if he had let the doctor take off his arm whether he would have made it or not," Cole said, trying to ease the conflict he saw roiling in her eyes.

"His pride . . . ," she said, and turned and tilted her face toward the sun, her eyes closed.

"He didn't want to come home and have you see him without his arm," Cole said. "I can understand that."

She turned suddenly. "He must have hated me terribly."

"No, he didn't hate you, Anna. He loved you. That's the message he asked me to deliver. He told me to tell you that he was sorry he couldn't love you enough."

She tried to blink back the tears. "If it was love," she said, her words faltering like young birds wrestling to be free from their nest, "then why did it grow so cold in our hearts? And why did he not show me his love and let my own die?"

"I can't answer that."

"No, of course you can't. You weren't here, were you?"

To Cole it sounded like an accusation, but a bitter heart is capable of almost anything. And right that moment, he knew her heart was grievous, a wounded thing, wounded by unspoken words, unrealized dreams. And he was certain much of that bitter wounded heart had begun its suffering the very night her father came and took their child from her.

"You must leave now," she said. "You must leave and never come back."

"I can't do that, Anna."

"You must."

"No. There is something I need to ask you about."

She knew the question before Cole voiced it. He could see the pain shadow itself behind the bitterness in her eyes. "Don't ask me," she said.

"I have to."

"Whatever he told you. . . ."

Cole took her by the shoulders and the feeling of her traveled the length of his arms and crept into his heart like a shadow. "I need to know about our son," he said.

Cole could feel her go weak in his arms, then stiffen as she tried to pull free of him. "Jimmy told you a lie."

"He was on his deathbed, Anna."

A sound caught in her throat and she choked it back. "Please. Please don't ask this of me."

191

"I need to know. I've lost one son already, Anna. Don't make me lose another without knowing."

She pulled free, turned her back to Cole, and folded her arms defiantly across her chest.

"Why didn't you tell me?"

Without turning around, she said: "How was I to tell you anything? You had already fled the Nations by the time he was born."

It was a shame Cole still carried—that he hadn't stopped to tell her before he left, or the reason why he was leaving.

"If you really loved me," she said, "you wouldn't have left. Loving someone doesn't mean leaving them."

"You're right, Anna. I made a bad mistake and let your daddy influence me and get me to believing I wasn't worthy of you."

She turned, her eyes wet and bright and full of anger.

"I'm a different man now than I was then. I was just a greenstick deputy without two nickels to rub together and a hat full of dreams. Your daddy was right not to let me have at you but I was wrong for listening to him. We all made mistakes, but that doesn't mean we have to keep on making them."

"My father was a hateful man," she said. "Full of pride just like Jimmy, and it cost him everything, just like Jimmy."

"He took the infant," Cole said.

Her eyes narrowed at the painful remembrance of that night. "I will always hate him for that."

"Jimmy told me something else about that night," Cole said. "He told me that your father gave the boy to a woman who once worked for him."

Tears coursed her cheeks.

"Rudina . . . ," she muttered. "Rudina said that he had died . . . just as my father said. . . ."

"Maybe she was simply trying to spare you," Cole said. "Your father could be a very intimidating man."

She slumped visibly. "It's hard to believe that she would lie to me."

"We'll go and ask her one more time," Cole suggested.

"No. Let it go. Too many years have passed."

"What difference does that make?"

She sobbed, beat her fists into his chest. "I don't think I can stand to know," she wept. "I don't think I can stand one more moment of heartache. . . ."

"If you know, you can reach a peace within yourself."

"You mean that you can find peace for *yourself*," she said, her words vindictive, angry.

"Yes, that, too."

She pulled free of him again and went into the house, and Cole followed her.

"Anna, you could have told me about this the last time we were together," he said, staring at the bed in the corner, remembering that afternoon not so long ago when their passion almost overcame the years of separation and washed away time.

"I would have never told you," she said. "Especially not then."

They sat and drank coffee and talked and the hours slipped by and the light shifted from one side of the room to the other, then grew dim. They had to light lamps. They talked about Jimmy and about the child and her father and all the years of hatred she had stored up in her heart. She talked about the long nights of wondering: "Do you know what it is like to have the two people you love most missing from your life?"

"Yes." Cole told her about his late wife and infant son who had both died of the milk sickness and how he had drifted for years with a hole in his heart the size of a fist. "Yes, I know what it's like, Anna. And they weren't the only ones that I missed during that time."

The words bled them of some of the heartache and bitterness and anger that had festered in all those years, but the words did not cleanse them in the blooding completely, and traces of memory and pain still lingered.

"I named him in my heart," she said at one point.

"What did you name him?"

"Thomas," she said. "I named him Thomas."

"Why Thomas?"

She shook her head slightly. "I just thought it was a good name."

"It is a good name."

Night fell against the windows.

"I want to find out what happened to him, Anna. If you don't want to know, I won't tell you, but I need to know."

She sat for a long time in silence, and he sat there, staring at her across the blackened lamp chimney that held a single yellow flame burning from the wick.

"We will go and see Rudina tomorrow," she said at last.

"Good."

"Now I must be alone with my thoughts."

"I understand," Cole said. "I'll ride back to Talaquah and come for you in the morning."

He wanted to kiss her, to kiss away the stains on her cheeks where her tears had dried, but he didn't because he didn't think she wanted him to do it. It was one of those moments where all the intimacy you've shared with someone seems a disadvantage. He said good night and rode back to town in the dark. The night was as black as he'd ever seen it and his sense of loneliness as great.

Chapter Twenty-Eight

Clarence Bellringer was drunk, his mind thick with dope. He'd brought back from Huang Yü's an Oriental girl whose skin was the color of dusk. He'd paid Huang Yü $25 for the privilege of her company and drove her home in his outlandish blue wagon. She was young and pretty and had sadly sweet eyes that caused him to want to weep inside each time he looked at her. Her name was Mai Ling (he thought it meant lotus flower) and he liked the sound of it when she said it.

He set a table for dinner for her and had her sit next to him and they ate like proper guests at a wedding feast, and he spoke to her in Mandarin and told her how beautiful she was and what an honor it was for him to share her company. All the while he told her these things, she offered him coy glances that turned his heart over and over with great affection for her.

"You are as lovely as sunrise, my dear," he said. Her almost innocent eyes were not diminished by the fact they glittered with the dope that ran through her veins. His own blood was thick with dope as well and it seemed to him a perfect way to be—in this near languid state with such a beautiful creature as she—the entire future awaiting them.

"Care for some capon?" he asked, and spilled his glass of wine in reaching for it, then laughed at the spilling.

She demurred, but he cut the small birds anyway, and served the meat on gilded plates that had been brought from Europe on a sailing schooner by some great aunt of his. They ate, and he fondled her hand beneath the table, and she continued to cast him shy glances with her almond-shaped eyes as he told her of himself, his past, medical school, gambling, whoring in South America, gold fields, the constellations, and all manner of things that ran through his mind. Some of the things he was positive she knew nothing about, but, nonetheless, he thought it important to tell her of these things, for he had in the hours between first meeting her in the Chinaman's dope den and this very moment determined that he would marry her. Why, he had no earthly idea, except that he was fawningly and madly taken by her beauty and youth and innocence. She was an impoverished child, enslaved and not in charge of her own affairs, and he'd decided amid the languor that she deserved better than the hand the gods had dealt her. And hadn't he much to give? Yes! He would free her of the yellow bastard and give her everything he owned!

"You are a dove," he said, interrupting himself while in the middle of a treatise on French politics, the sordid feelings having ambushed him each time he took full stock of her physical beauty. He kissed the knuckles of her hand. The bones were smooth and delicate against his lips and he lingered over them, her dusky warmth filling his senses. "It's time I married," he said.

She glanced upward at him.

"Will you marry me, my lotus flower, and give me sons?"

He could see the doubt in her eyes. He nibbled her knuckles. She tittered. He felt great waves of passion for her.

"I love you," he said. "Can you understand how I can in such short time?"

She smiled such that it turned his heart over again.

"I will give you my fortune, make you a queen of all you survey, buy you from that yellow bastard, Huang Yü, and give you a proper reputation," he declared.

She leaned toward him and kissed his cheek and whispered her affections for him and it stirred his passion even greater, if that was possible, and he stood and lifted her in his arms and carried her up the staircase, where he placed her on the big four-poster bed and began to unloose his galluses.

She lay there, as innocent and quiet and gentle as a floating lotus flower—as lovely as dawn on water. He suddenly felt rueful, his trousers partway down his legs, still holding them by the galluses.

"I shame you," he said. "I'm a rude Occidental who has no right to thrust myself on you, to burden you with my sins. . . ."

She reached for him.

He felt the flames of his desire re-ignite and scorch his loins. "I'm not worthy of you, my flower."

He felt as though he was walking on the very edge of a tall building. He fell to his knees and pressed his face to her lap. She took his head in her hands and whispered something soothing, muffled as it was to him there in the folds of her skirts, and stroked his hair gently. "I would give everything to have you," he said. "Everything!"

She moaned. Her scent was strong, womanly, devastating.

He rose, finished shedding his trousers, removed his shirt, and stood before her naked, stripped of any pretenses except for those in his rueful heart. She closed her eyes as his hands slid her skirts upward over her legs. Her lips parted to reveal her fine small teeth. It made him want her more.

Then something shattered the moment. The opening of the front door below. "What in hell!" He stumbled, trying to find his trousers. She opened her eyes, startled.

He turned away from her, her skirts still lifted past her knees, his eyes unwilling to abandon her beauty completely. He heard commotion in the foyer, the curses of men, the stomping of boots, and reached in a bedside drawer for the small pearl-handled revolver he kept there—the one he often in his darkest hours contemplated using on himself.

She shuddered on the bed, her eyes full of fright and uncertainty, and he quickly pointed toward a wardrobe and told her to get in it. She didn't understand. He lifted her from the bed and led her to it and urged her inside.

He turned in time to see dark faces at the bedroom door. *Indians,* he thought. *What the hell are Indians doing in my house?*

Then a white man appeared amid them, pushing his way through, saying: "You one of them god-damn' deputies?"

He fired the pistol but his aim was untrue and missed its mark and splintered a piece of the wainscoting, and at once the men in the doorway fired their weapons into him and he fell, sure that he was dying, the pain so terrible it couldn't be any other way. He clutched the bedding as he slumped to the floor and pulled the coverlet over him, Mai Ling's scent still within its folds, and he wondered why it was these men had come and shot him, then remembered the big blue wagon he'd traded to the lawman and the woman. *That is what it must have been,* he thought, his mind lucid now, full of a clarity he'd not known in years. *These wild bastards think that I am one of them, that I am John Henry Cole or that poor devil, Jimmy Wild Bird.* The thought seemed at once laughable and pitiful. Of all the endings he could have conceived, this wasn't one of them.

As canny as cats they dragged the woman from the wardrobe and turned her this way and that and grabbed at her, and the white man leaned down close to Clarence Bellringer and said: "Chinese bitch, eh. You like 'em yellow?"

Clarence gargled on his blood, spit it into the man's face, and the man backhanded him.

"Where's the others?" the man said, wiping the bloody froth from his face.

"Burning in hell, same as you will be," Clarence said,

surprised at his own defiance.

They shoved Mai Ling to the carpet so that her face was next to his and one of them took a knife and put it to her throat, and the white man said: "You want to be a ass? You want to act tough and protect your pals? How 'bout we rape her with our knives, then cut this bitch's throat?"

Clarence looked into those sad sweet eyes of Mai Ling's and saw the empty landscape of his life, a wasteland upon which he had trod and ending there in their wet brown innocence. That yellow bastard, Huang Yü, had probably been prostituting her since she was ten years old and she had never known a childhood and the beauty of a child's dreams. And now she would never know. "Let her go and I'll tell you," he said.

The man's breath was rancid and he smiled and said—"Sure, *amigo*."—and said something to the Indian, who took the knife away. Mai Ling lay there like a wounded doe.

"You best hurry and tell us," the white man said. "You're runnin' plum out of blood, partner."

"Talaquah. . . ."

"Talaquah." The man leaned closer. "How many?"

"Just one."

"One, eh. What's he look like? How we gonna know him we find him?"

"He's got a limp from being gunshot. Big man. White, like you. Reddish brown beard . . . mustaches. . . ."

"Shit," the white man said, and stood, pulling Mai Ling up by the hair.

Clarence knew it was a lost hand when he'd played it, but he'd had to play it anyway in the barest hope they weren't really interested in her, that they would show a shred of decency toward a girl who had never known any real kindness. But he could see they were neither kind nor prescient men. He pulled the pistol from under the coverlet—her scent delirious in his

199

brain—just as one of them ripped her dress down the middle.

He shot her through the forehead, knowing he couldn't kill all of them before they finished him, and the girl would suffer their outrage before they took her life. This way, she wouldn't have to suffer. She died as if struck by a thunderbolt and fell on the carpet next to him, the innocence and light gone out of her eyes like a candle flame extinguished by the wind. The dead eyes stared into his own and he silently professed his love to her. He heard the men curse, then the world went white.

CHAPTER TWENTY-NINE

Anna rode a black and John Henry Cole rode a bay. She said the bay had been one of Jimmy's favorites. Bone Blue and Rudina lived a mile outside of Talaquah in a long, low, log house with gardens that were in bloom. Squash blossoms and black-eyed Susans and buttercups tilted toward the sun, their stems bending to the gentle breezes. Cole could smell the river that flowed beyond the gardens and the copse of trees beyond them.

Bone Blue was hasping the forehoof of a big gelding. He wore a leather apron and his face was dark with sweat.

"That's Rudina," Anna said, nodding toward a woman who bent to the hoe in one of the gardens. Bone Blue dropped the hoof of the gelding and straightened when he saw them riding up. It didn't take a mind-reader to know what was going on behind those dark eyes of his as he stood there, waiting. His face was knotted and his hands hung by his sides. He was a big man who leaned slightly to the right as though he weighed more on that side than he did the other.

"Bone," Anna said, when they halted their horses in front of him.

He looked at her, then back at Cole. "I'm sorry as hell about Jimmy," he said without looking at her.

"I know," she said. "You were his best friend in the world."

"Since he was a kid," he said.

"I need to speak with Rudina, Bone."

He turned slightly to look at his wife, who hadn't heard them ride up, or at least had given no indication that she had. "What about?" Bone said.

"The child."

A spot just under his left eye twitched. He shook his head slightly and said: "Why not leave it be, Anna? That's all been such a long time ago."

"Don't do this, Bone."

He looked at her finally, taking his gaze from Cole. "Dammit, gal."

Anna slid from her horse and walked out toward the garden while Cole sat his saddle, watching. Finally Rudina turned, holding her hoe by the handle as though she needed it for support, the blade resting among the vegetables that were recently sprung from the earth: turnips and squash and beans.

"Ain't bad enough you had to come back without Jimmy," Bone said. "Now look what you've stirred up."

"You know about what happened," Cole said. "I'd like to hear about it."

He shook his head. "It happened long before Rudina and me got hitched. I don't know anything about it."

"You know something," Cole insisted.

"I know what you know. Nothing."

"Then why try and stop Anna from talking to your wife?"

"We don't need more trouble than what we got already. And we don't need to be dragging up the past."

Cole saw Anna approach her cousin, saw them standing there, Anna saying something to her, the other woman's face dark under the shadows of her hat, but saw, too, the way she turned her head slightly to look in Cole's direction.

"I've been thinking," Bone said.

"About what?"

"About me and you going after them god-damn' bastards."

"They could be scattered from here to the Canadian border," Cole said.

"You don't want to go after them, that it?"

Cole looked at Bone for a long hard moment, looked to the garden where Anna and her cousin were walking off now toward the trees in the direction of the river that Cole had smelled, riding up. "I plan on going after them," he said. "I don't need your help." Cole saw some of the grit go out of Bone's jaw.

"Time I got off my fat ass and did something," he said. "I'm pure wore out from sitting around here seeing my friends brought back in wagons . . . or not brought back at all."

Cole dismounted, took Anna's horse and his over to the water tank to let them drink. While they were drinking, he rolled himself a shuck and smoked it and watched the wind carry away the smoke.

"You don't think I'm up to the task, that it?" Bone said, coming to stand across from Cole, one boot propped on the edge of the tank.

Cole could see their reflections in the water like floating ghosts, and he thought to himself: *That's what we are, ghosts . . . all of us. Ghosts that are passing through this life to the next, Jimmy, Anna, Bone, Joe Digger, me.* "There's going to come a rain," he said, now looking off toward the west where the sky was building itself into a summer storm.

"I've been hunting and killing men in these Nations long before you white boys came over from Fort Smith," Bone said. A small white scar showed itself just under his chin like a piece of fingernail.

"How old are you, Bone?"

"I'll be fifty, Christmas day. Why the hell you ask?"

"You love that woman, the life you've made for yourselves here?"

He turned, saw that Anna and Rudina had disappeared down

a slope beyond the stand of walnut trees. "Love her? Hell, she's the only woman I ever loved."

"Then why bring her grief."

"What the hell you talking about?"

"They'll kill you, Bone. Hell, they'll probably kill me, too. Difference is, I don't have a woman like that, someone who wouldn't know what to do if I wasn't here. You really want your wife to be a widow before her time?"

He swallowed hard, stared off toward the trees. "We all die sometime," he said.

"True enough, but nothing says you have to hurry it along."

"I owe my friend."

"So do I. So let me take care of it."

"Shit," he said, then took his boot off the tank and removed his hat and looked into it like he'd misplaced something important and it might be in there. "What sort of man would I be, I didn't get vengeance for Jimmy?"

"An alive one," Cole said.

"I ain't afraid to die for what's right."

"What's right is you stay here and take care of your wife."

"God damn if I don't need a drink. You?"

Cole waited while Bone went to a springhouse and came back with a crock, dripping water and stoppered with a cork.

"Illegal," he said. "I buy it off a whiskey drummer named Ike who comes through here about every three months. I arrested him once and the deputies over in Fort Smith arrested him three or four times. But he keeps coming back 'cause it's all he knows how to do to make a living. So I buy his whiskey now and save myself the expense and time of jailing him."

He handed Cole the crock and Cole took a pull, and handed it back. "Tastes like kerosene," he said.

"Yeah, don't it."

★ ★ ★ ★ ★

An hour passed before Anna and Rudina came back to the house. Rudina didn't look at Cole, but even so he could see her eyes were rimmed red and so were Anna's. Bone took his wife by the arm and led her into the house.

"You OK?" Cole asked Anna.

She shook her head. "It's as Jimmy said . . . Thomas was given to my father's housekeeper. He might still be alive. . . ." Her words were like a shiver down Cole's spine.

"Where did this woman take him?"

She shrugged and said: "Walk with me for a bit, John Henry."

They walked through a pasture of wildflowers and a pair of cardinals chased each other through the trees. The first stiff winds from the approaching storm caught Anna's skirts and ruffled them.

"The woman took him to Ardmore," she said, her voice quavering. "Rudina says that he set her up with a house over there and. . . ." Her voice broke with emotion. Cole guided Anna to a fallen log and they sat on it. She looked at Cole, her eyes wet and full of betrayal. "She was more than just his housekeeper." Cole waited for her to regain her composure and tell the rest of the story. "I remember the woman and the story Papa told me of why she left and I never connected the two events of her leaving right after our son was born. He said that she left because her mother was dying and she needed to go and care for her. That's what I remember my father telling my mother and me."

"You think your mother knew about it, too?" Cole asked.

"Yes. She must have died with the bitterness still in her."

"I'm sorry, Anna."

"I want to go and see if we can find him, John Henry."

"Then we go to Ardmore. We go as soon as you're ready."

"Yes. . . ." Cole started to stand but she took hold of his

sleeve. "I'm afraid, John Henry."

"He's your son, Anna. Our son."

"What if . . . ?"

"We won't know until we go and find him."

"But if he's yet alive . . . who knows the stories he's been told about us?"

"Time he learned the truth. We owe him that much."

She leaned against Cole, her tears soaking the front of his shirt, and she felt frail in his arms and he wanted to protect her but wasn't sure he could even as his own heart seemed to fail him. The thought of seeing a son he had never known he had until a few days ago was daunting. She kissed his cheek and said: "Let's go to Ardmore."

They stopped at the house and told Bone and Rudina they were leaving, and Bone said to Cole: "Surely you'll stay to dinner so's we can talk about certain matters, me and you?"

Cole replied that they wouldn't and his face grew dark and troubled. "You know how I feel," he said. He looked at the woman by his side. "There's no dishonor in doing your duty, Bone. I think you know what that is."

They started to mount and Cole was holding Anna's stirrup for her when Bone came out of the house, carrying a nickel-plated Winchester with a tang rear-sight and brass studs in the stock. "Take this," he said.

"What for?"

"I got it loaded with notched bullets, cut crosses in the heads so when they hit, they flatten out and do some real damage. You take it and do those boys some damage."

Cole understood his meaning and took the rifle, sliding his own from the boot in exchange.

"She shoots a hair to the left," was the last thing Bone said as he shook hands with Cole.

They rode off.

About a mile away from the house, Anna broke their silence: "Looks like a storm is coming."

"Looks like," Cole agreed. The storm felt as though it were inside him already.

CHAPTER THIRTY

Pablo had dreams that night, there under the hard rain that soaked the blankets he had strung between two saplings to make a crude tent. The water dripped through and fell onto his face like cold tears, and he dreamed of his wife, dreamed she had come looking for him through the trees, her dress torn, her lips bloody, a ragged wound above her breasts. In the dream he tried to rise and go to her but he couldn't move his arms or legs—they felt like stone, and she stood there at the edge of the tree line calling out to him, her arms extended, cut marks from a knife slashed into her flesh like small red crucifixes. Then a man in white robes came and sat on a rock near his feet and said: "Are you ready to go with me, Pablo?" He awakened with a start, the water running off his face as his heart staggered inside his chest.

"María!" he called. The lightning flashed across the sky and lit the trees and there was no one there. He cursed the whiskey he'd drunk earlier to help him sleep and to take away the pain in his bones from having ridden all day. He cursed his luck at having lost the trail of the men because the rain had come and washed away their tracks. He cursed the souls of the men. And he cursed himself for being such an old fool.

His clothing was soaked and the cold rain caused him to cough. He felt the death coming in him. He reached for the whiskey bottle, saw that it was empty, and cursed its emptiness. He stood and took the blankets and saddled the horse and rode into Tulsa, arriving the next morning about dawn. That is where he saw the man in the box.

There in the window of a funeral parlor a dead man was propped up in an open coffin. Pablo stopped his horse and looked for a time through the plate glass at the man whose eyes were half closed and whose hair was parted and combed into wet strands. The man was dressed in a green checked suit and his hands were crossed and tied at the wrists with a bit of twine. There was black bunting around the window and the dawn sun struck the glass and reflected Pablo's own image superimposed over that of the dead man. Pablo wondered if it might be an omen.

He rode on, found a small café, and dismounted. Three or four people were eating their breakfasts and they looked up when he entered, then went back to eating. He sat down at an empty table and soon a man came over and asked him what he would have, and he said he'd like a cup of coffee and something to eat, knowing he had no money to pay for it, and laid his rifle across the table. The man said—"Sure, sure."—and went into the kitchen and came back in a moment with his coffee, and set it before him, saying that his breakfast would be out in a few minutes.

"I saw a dead man in a box," Pablo said.

"Yes, that is Clarence Bellringer. He used to be a doctor of sorts until the other day some men shot and killed him and a young Chinese whore."

"Why did these men shoot him?" Pablo asked, sensing something important.

The man shrugged. "Who knows?" The man wore an apron around his thick waist and garters on his sleeves. And Pablo noticed, too, that his hair was combed and parted down the middle like that of the dead man. When the man saw that his answer didn't seem adequate to suit Pablo he said: "They just rode in and found him in his house and shot him to pieces."

"And the woman?"

The man shook his head. "God, you don't want to know what they did to her."

Pablo knew for certain then that they were the men he was looking for. "Do you know which way these men went when they left here?"

The man shook his head. "No, sir, I was fishing the day it happened. Caught three big river cats and a dogfish." Pablo felt the disappointment all the way into his bones. The man must have sensed Pablo's disappointment, for he said: "Fat Flora said she saw 'em."

"Who is Fat Flora?"

"The baker's wife. Sees everything. All she does is sit and watch what goes on and eat. Man can't take a leak out behind the barn she don't see it."

"Where does this woman live?"

"With the baker, of course."

"Where does he live?"

"Up the street, around the corner to your right. You can smell it a block before you get there."

"Thank you," Pablo said, and rose to leave.

"Ain't you going to drink your coffee, stay and eat your breakfast?"

"No. I have no money to pay for it."

The man looked at the coffee, looked at Pablo, at the poor way he was dressed. "Hell," he said. "This here part of the country is getting run over with bums."

"I'm not a bum, *señor.*"

The man looked at him. "You know how to wash dishes?"

"Wash dishes?"

"Yes, do you know how and are you willing to wash some dishes for your breakfast?"

"I need to go see the baker's wife," Pablo said, adjusting his torn straw sombrero on his head again.

"Well, it's up to you, hoss."

Pablo could smell the food frying in the kitchen and his stomach turned over. "How many dishes?"

"A sink full," the man said. "My dishwasher fell off a roof and broke his leg."

"What was he doing on a roof?" Pablo asked.

"Trying to fix it so's it wouldn't leak in on him."

"Oh."

"You want to eat or not?"

Pablo sat back down, took off his hat, and placed it on the seat next to him, then took a sip of the coffee. "OK, then," he said.

"Good, I'll bring out your plate."

After Pablo ate and washed the sink of dishes, he walked down the street to the baker's house feeling much better. The sun was rising from behind a low bank of silvery clouds and its rays felt warm on his skin. Maybe he would live long enough to find the men and finish his business with them after all.

The baker's wife sat eating a pastry out front of the store. She was fat, just as the man had said. Pablo could see the baker through the window; he was bent to an open oven, taking out a tray of breads.

"I am told that you saw the men who shot *Señor* Bellringer," Pablo said without the formality of an introduction.

The woman looked up at him with sugar on her lips. "You bet I did. Four of them. Meanest-looking dogs I ever laid eyes on in this town. Injuns, looked like. Except one could have been a white man. Hard to tell, they was all so dirty filthy."

Pablo's blood stirred. "Did you see which way they went when they left here?"

"That way," she said, pointing with her chin. "They took the road toward Talaquah."

"When exactly did all this happen?"

"Two days ago. Before it rained. Lord, you should 'a' seen what they did to that poor China girl he had in the house with him. . . ."

Pablo tried not to think about it. He saw the fat woman staring at him as she stuffed the rest of the pastry into her mouth. She was watching him like he might be her next meal. He was already on the trail of the men in his thoughts. This time they would not escape. And his blood was the hunter's blood once more.

CHAPTER THIRTY-ONE

John Henry Cole and Anna Wild Bird stopped often to rest the horses and rest themselves. Cole's leg still ached from the bullet wound, and when Anna asked him about it, he told her he was simply getting too old to carry another man's lead around in him. She didn't see the humor in it.

They stopped the first night at a small town they didn't know the name of but the lights of which they had seen a mile out. Cole located a boarding house run by a woman who let them know right off that she was a Christian woman and not pleased to be troubled after dark by wayfaring strangers.

"Got one room I could rent you," she said after taking stock of them, then asked if they were married. Cole started to say something, but Anna cut him off.

"We were just," she said.

The woman saw the silver wedding band on Anna's finger. "That's good, because I don't let out my rooms to trash or sinners. Man sleeps with a woman, they best be married if they want a room at my place."

Cole paid her $3 and took the key. When they entered their room, Cole lit the lamp next to the bed. It was a small bed.

"I can make a pallet on the floor," he said.

Anna turned her back to him and began to unbutton her shirt. "No," she said. "I won't have you sleeping on the floor like an old hound."

"I just thought. . . ."

213

"Please, don't say anything, John Henry."

Cole removed his hat, sat on a chair, and took off his boots and socks, and watched her finish undressing. She stood for a moment, silent, wearing only her underwear, bloomers and a chemise—then she turned slowly, saw that Cole was looking at her. "This reminds me of our first time in that hotel, do you remember?" she said, her face half-hidden by the shadows.

"How could I forget?"

She crossed the room, took his face in her hands, and looked down at him. Her countenance was soft, the eyes sadly sweet as they always were, as they had been that first night all those years ago. Her black hair framed her high cheek bones and he kissed her hands, and she closed her eyes, and he could feel her shudder as he stood up and took her in his arms. "We don't have to. . . ."

She kissed him on the lips. The kiss was as light and delicate as snow falling. "I need you to hold me tonight, John Henry," she whispered. "I just need to be held."

He finished undressing and slipped into the small bed next to her, and she curled into him and he held her and held her until he could feel the even breathing of her sleep, and he held her still. Throughout the night he dozed and awakened to make sure she was still there, and at one point he heard rain lashing the windows and saw flashes of lightning and felt the room shake from the thunder. The thunderclap awakened her and she bolted upright, startled, uncertain of where she was, and clung to him and whispered his name, and when he said—"Yes."—she kissed him again, and sank back down into the bedding, curling herself in his arms.

The next morning they went down and ate breakfast at a long table with the other boarders, and the landlady who sat across from Anna and Cole looked at Anna and said: "You look happy."

Anna only shrugged her shoulders.

The woman wished them well on their journey.

A few days later they arrived in Ardmore just as the sun was beginning to settle into a flaming orange ball beyond a distant line of trees.

"This woman," Cole said. "Do you know where we'll find her?"

"Her name is Naomi Little Horse and Rudina said that she heard she was working as a fortune-teller."

"Then she shouldn't be hard to locate."

"If she is still here in Ardmore," Anna said, the sound of near desperation in her voice.

They saw a group of children playing baseball in a vacant lot, and Cole called to one of them, a red-headed boy wearing short pants, and asked him where they could find the local sheriff. He laughed and said: "Cemetery, mister. Ole Bob passed on yesterday."

"Well, is there someone who's taken his place, kid?"

"Burly, maybe. Burly's a bit tetched, but he was ole Bob's deputy."

Cole handed the kid a nickel and asked him where they would find this deputy, Burly, and the kid said: "Most likely skinned out in Madam Foot's hurdy-gurdy which is south of that red building yonder. She's a whore, Madam Foot is."

They rode south of the red building and saw the sign above a door, advertising *MADAM FOOT'S HOUSE OF PLEASURE.*

"You want to wait here while I go in and call on Madam?" Cole said to Anna.

"Sure."

He handed her the reins to his horse and went in.

A skinny woman with a bad cough and worse teeth approached Cole once inside and asked if she would do.

"Do for what?" Cole said.

"You're too old to be a virgin, mister. What do you think men come in here for?"

"Not looking for company," he said. "I'm looking for a man named Burly."

"Oh, hell," she said. "Burly's taking a bath with Eva." She pointed toward a door. Cole went in without bothering to knock.

A fat man and a fatter woman were crammed into a zinc tub full of water and soap bubbles. A stoppered whiskey bottle floated atop the water between them. "Hey there!" the man said. "This is a private party!"

"You Burly?"

"Who the hell's asking?"

"I'm asking. You him?"

Burly was pink as a pig, hairless except for a small Van Dyke on his chin, and brushy eyebrows. One of his eyes was offset.

"What if I am?" he said. "You ain't wanting a gunfight, are you?"

"Looking for a woman name of Naomi Little Horse, told she might work as a fortune-teller around here. You ever hear of her?"

He looked at the woman in the tub with him, then back at Cole. Cole could see then she was cross-eyed, too. Burly blinked. It made him look stupid. "You mean that old Indian witch?" he said.

"Then you know where I can find her."

"Lives out on the west edge of town in a yeller house with blue shutters. Keeps a goat in the yard which she bleeds to make potions with."

Cole started to turn to leave.

"Hey, mister," the man said.

"What?" It was hard to know which eye to look at.

"They say that goat used to be her feller till she caught him cheating on her. I wouldn't go out there and piss her off or

216

★ ★ ★ ★ ★

Book V

★ ★ ★ ★ ★

CHAPTER THIRTY-TWO

Rain sluiced from the gutters and dripped from the trees and the sky was dark gray and swollen and the wind was cold. *Middle of July,* Bone Blue thought, *and cold enough to make my back hurt.* It still troubled him greatly that he had not gone with the white man, John Henry Cole, in search of the killers of his best friend. For two days he did nothing but sit around and think about it and watch the efforts of his wife in her garden, or as she cooked their meals and washed his clothes. Junior Dove had ridden out once from town and said that someone had stolen old man Teal's chestnut horse and wasn't he going to go look for it?

"Not today," Bone had said. "Maybe not tomorrow, either."

Junior Dove had looked duly perplexed and said: "Well, ain't it your job, Bone? Ain't that what you get paid for?"

"You want to be the constable," Bone had said, "you're welcome to it, Junior."

Junior had toed the dirt and said: "Well, I ain't saying nothing against you, Bone. Hell, I know it ain't easy being a lawman, especially in these bad times. But you know Teal's blind as a bat and all he's got to his name is that chestnut and somebody's sure as hell stole it."

So Bone was sitting around thinking about Jimmy and thinking about Rudina and thinking about whether or not he ought to go and find Teal's chestnut horse when the rain came and washed away all of his will to carry out his duties.

"I've been thinking," he said to Rudina, who now stood at the stove stirring a mutton stew she had put together earlier that morning.

"About what?" she said without bothering to turn and look at him.

"That maybe we ought to move."

"Move?"

"Yes. I'm sorta getting wore out on this place."

She stopped stirring and turned to look at him, the ladle still in her hand. "Well, where would we go, Bone? All our friends are right here in Talaquah. Your job is right here in Talaquah."

"All my friends are dead and in the ground right here in Talaquah," Bone said. "That's all I know about anything. And this job I got ain't much more than running around finding somebody's stole horse or settling squabbles between Jack Finch and his wife every time they get the notion to get drunk and start in on each other. Hell, Rudina, I'm wore out on this life and this place."

She sat down across from him then, weary as she'd ever felt; he could see the weariness in her eyes, in the darkness around them, in the slump of her shoulders.

"Bone, I don't want to leave Talaquah. We're too old to start over again."

He knew she was right, but knowing she was right didn't ease the itch he had in him to be shut of this place, the ghosts that lingered around it, men he'd known in life, had gambled and fished with and drank with. He thought about Jimmy Wild Bird, buried somewhere in some unmarked grave like as though he'd never even existed. Now Anna was gone off looking for a lost or stolen child. Anna and Jimmy were both gone from their lives, the last best friends they had. It was like the world was emptying out of people he knew and he and Rudina were the last ones left on earth.

"I know what I'm going to do, then," he said, for the thought had suddenly occurred to him as he sat there, like a lightning bolt, like God had spoken in his ear.

"What?"

"I'm going to go get Jimmy and bring him home."

"Go get him?"

"Yes. He belongs here."

He saw the way her face knotted in anguish from his announcement, but it didn't matter because this was one thing he had to do. Of all the things he had ever done in life, none of them seemed to him as important as this one thing. He knew he had to do it, that he had no choice. "I'll take the wagon, drive over to Tulsa, locate where he's buried, and bring him back. Put him in the family cemetery, get him a headstone. A man's life ought to at least count for something. What he's done, what he stood for, should not be so easily forgot."

"Nobody's going to forget Jimmy," Rudina said, rubbing her hands together as though they ached.

"What about twenty years from now?"

She slowly nodded. He knew that look when she gave up trying to argue with him. They both sat there for a time, listening to the rain drum on the tin roof of the cabin, then Bone stood and walked into their bedroom and packed an extra shirt and some socks into a valise and carried it out into the kitchen and set it on the table.

"I won't be gone long," he said. "Five, six days at the outside."

She wouldn't look at him.

"What's wrong?" he said.

"They should rename this town the City of Widows," she said.

"You're not a widow."

"I have a feeling I am about to become one soon."

"Don't be foolish, woman. I'm just going to go get my friend and bring him back."

"The rain . . . ," she said.

"What about it?"

"Something bad is going to happen."

"No. All the bad things have already happened. There's nothing left for anything bad to happen to."

She wept. He tried comforting her. She went in and lay across the bed and he went in and sat next to her for a time, trying to console her.

"Stay," she said.

"I can't."

She sat up, wiped the tears from her eyes, and said: "Then I will not cry for you any more." She stood and walked into the kitchen and resumed her watch over the mutton stew.

He donned a slicker that was hanging by the door and tugged his hat down tightly on his head before taking the valise and going out. Mud was to the top of his boots and it sucked at them as he crossed the yard to the lean-to where he kept the spring wagon. It would take longer going to Tulsa by wagon than by horse, but he needed the wagon to bring back his friend. He was hitching the horse into the traces when he saw the ghosts in the rain, sitting there astride played-out ponies. And somehow he knew that they were the men who had killed his friend.

CHAPTER THIRTY-THREE

"What will we do now, John Henry?" Anna asked when she'd regained her composure.

They were sitting in a café having coffee, watching the rain, and the rain and the gloom seemed appropriate for the way they were feeling. "I need to get you back to Talaquah, then go look for those boys before it's too late."

"How do you know it's not already too late?"

"I don't. But I'm hoping it isn't."

Cole saw the look of despair in her eyes as she stared at her reflection in the rain-slicked glass. He thought about the times of their lives, the directions they had taken, the secrets kept, and how it all put this strange sense of uneasiness between him and Anna. He loved her still, and he thought she still loved him, but everything that had transpired in the last few days had changed them in ways they couldn't fix any easier than they could turn back those days to a better time.

"Look," he said, "this wasn't your fault."

"Then why does it feel that way?"

He rolled a shuck and smoked it and asked her if she was up to a return trip so soon.

"I feel weary," she said.

"Maybe you should stay in Ardmore a while and rest, let me go on and see if I can locate them."

"No. I will go back with you to Talaquah. I will go with you as far as I can, as far as you'll let me. . . ."

There was a stage line across the street, and Cole walked over and asked if they had a run going to Talaquah, and the man said one was leaving in an hour. Cole bought a pair of tickets, then walked down to the livery and sold the horses and saddles. He knew Anna wasn't up to another long horseback ride.

"It's a straight-through haul," Cole said when he told her about taking the stage. "We'll be back in Talaquah tomorrow night. You sure you don't want to stay over for a while?"

She simply looked at him, her sad eyes full of anguish.

An hour later they were aboard the mud wagon in close quarters with a Cherokee farmer, his large, bosomy wife, and their two children and an infant who suckled at the woman's breast. The farmer looked at Anna and Cole, saw the difference in their color, and showed his disapproval without saying a word. But Cole no longer cared what anybody thought about them.

They rode like that, rocking over the rutted, mud-slathered road from stage stop to stage stop, halting only long enough to change horses and for the driver and his partner to relieve themselves. They bought coffee and hardtack at one of the stage stops, and the farmer and his wife and children ate sandwiches wrapped in butcher paper that the farmer took from his coat pocket. They drank from a single canteen.

After hours of riding, cramped as they were, the stopping for the change of horses was a relief, allowing them the small pleasure of stretching their legs and backs. Cole knew it was hard on Anna, but he also knew her mind wasn't on the journey as much as it was on where the journey led and what lay at the end of the line.

During the night she slept, her head leaning on Cole's shoulder, and the farmer's children whimpered like restless kittens as they tried to sleep, too. Rain and darkness and a rocky road made miserable traveling companions.

Cole's mind kept turning over the possibility that the boy he'd shot back at Greasy Junction might well have been his son. How the hell could he have known that? He'd been weighing telling Anna about it ever since the witch woman had told them the story. But not knowing for certain whether it was Thomas he'd shot or not only seemed a cruel lash to lay on Anna at this point. The odds were one in four that he could have been the boy he had shot. The thought made his temples throb painfully. He dozed on and off from sheer weariness, and several times he had fitful dreams of a dead boy reaching out to him with a look of wonderment and pleading in his eyes, and Cole would wake with a start to the darkness of the interior of the mud wagon, wake to the snores of the farmer and his wife and the whimpering of their children and, his hands cold as ice.

Daylight came over the land in soft shades of increasing grayness. The rain had stopped and soon sunlight filtered through a crack in the sodden clouds that lay off to the east as they pulled into a stage stop. It seemed for several moments that they were still moving, the motion of the journey still riding in their blood.

Cole stepped down, helped Anna down, and then the farmer's children, as the farmer helped his wife, who was carrying the infant. The driver announced they could wash their hands and faces at the pump and buy breakfast inside the way station and that they'd be changing drivers for the next leg of the journey.

Anna and the farmer's wife and children headed off toward the privy. The farmer pulled a plug from his pocket and cut off a chew and pushed it inside his mouth, then chewed on it for a time before saying: "Some god-damn' ride, huh?"

Cole nodded, rolled himself a shuck.

"You don't remember me, do you?" he said.

Cole looked at him, shook his head. "Can't say I do."

"You used to be a deputy marshal out of Fort Smith," he said.

Cole nodded.

"You still?"

"No."

"Got tired of arresting poor-assed Indians?"

"Got shot," Cole said.

"Well, that's as good a reason as any. I guess a lot of you deputies get shot over here in the Nations."

Cole ignored the comment.

He rubbed his hands together working some heat or blood into them. " 'Member who it was that shot you?" he asked.

Cole looked at him, saw something familiar in the broad face. "Lucky?"

"I put on a few pounds since you seen me last," he said.

"That gal with the infant," Cole said. "She's not the woman who shot me."

He shook his head. "No, that ain't the same wife I had back then . . . the one that shot you. That was Alice. She died of tainted whiskey a month after she plugged you with that musket."

"That's too bad."

"I told her a bunch of times not to drink so much, but she was hell on liquor. A cross-eyed white son-of-a-bitch come through with snakehead liquor and was selling it cheap. Three, four others died besides Alice. We caught up with him and dragged him by his heels from our horses until he wasn't fit for dog food." He leaned and spat just as his family was coming back up from the privy.

"You ain't still sore at me 'cause she shot you, are you? I din't ask her to or nothing."

"No, Lucky, that was a long time ago and I'm sorry Alice ended up dying from tainted whiskey."

"Me, too," he said. "She was a pretty good screw. Hope you have better luck with your wife than I did with mine. Least you was smart enough to marry an Indian gal."

Cole didn't bother to tell him that Anna wasn't his wife.

The mud wagon made Talaquah by midnight. Cole said to Anna: "Do you want to ride out to see Bone tonight, or should we take a room and go in the morning?"

"Let's take a room," she said. "I'd hate to disturb him at this hour."

That night she lay, stiff and silent, in Cole's arms and he knew they'd been changed forever, and his heart was heavy as a stone in his chest because they had. He listened to her murmuring sleep and thought it sounded like the most lonesome wind blowing across the most lonesome prairie, and wept silently to the sound of it.

CHAPTER THIRTY-FOUR

Bone Blue moved with stealth back toward the cabin, but the riders saw him and spurred their mounts forward, cutting him off like a pack of gray wolves cutting out a deer, and he retreated back toward the lean-to. The rain blurred his vision, but he didn't need to see their faces to know who they were and what they wanted. "Murderers!" he called, hoping Rudina would hear his voice in time to look out and see the trouble sitting horses in her front yard and take refuge in the summer cellar. They sat there, looking in his direction through the veil of rain.

He had that big Schofield pistol and his Henry rifle and a box of shells for each and he swore an oath to himself he'd fire every last round into them. But as soon as he brought up the rifle, they were gone—like ghosts, like they'd never been there. What to do? Make a run for the house, or sit tight? His heart thumped so hard he could hear the blood beat in his ears.

How the hell did they come to be here? he wondered. Then he heard something moving, saw a shadow sliding along the north wall of the cabin, another slipping around back. *Oh, holy Jesus, they're going to get Rudina!* His shot seemed to shatter a world that, until this moment, had been stillborn, and he heard Rudina scream and thought: *My God, I didn't shoot her, did I?* He squatted there, fear gripping his gut, twisting inside him like a knife blade.

He heard the roar of a shotgun, then silence. Saw two shadows moving back from the cabin's walls in retreat. *Good for you, old girl, give 'em hell!* She hadn't retreated to the summer cellar—she'd taken up the shotgun he kept just inside the rear door. He snapped off three, four, maybe five shots at the retreating shadows. Then sat for a long time, listening to the rain. He was breathing hard, his chest felt full of fire. *Too god-damn' old for shoot-outs,* he told himself.

It was maybe a hundred yards from the lean-to to the cabin. A hundred long yards with nothing in between but the rain. He could go running up and crashing in through the door but with Rudina in there with that Hamilton double-barreled shotgun, she'd blast him to dog meat before she realized it was he. He could call out to her, but then they'd know he was coming and pick him off like a wild turkey. He thought about it a moment longer. *Hell, if I'm going to get shot, I'd just as soon it be my wife done it as those god-damn' bastards. I'd just as soon die in my own house instead of out here in the rain.* He hitched up his pants and made a run for it, bracing himself against the unseen bullets that would come out of the rain—a rain of bullets—and sloughed his way toward the cabin as fast as his legs could carry his bulk. He slipped in the mud once and fell and lost the Schofield, didn't bother to look for it, got up, and kept moving. Just as he hit the front porch, he shouted—"Don't shoot, woman, it's me!"—and burst through the door and landed hard on the floor in a heap. He rolled over and looked up into the twin black holes of the Hamilton. Rudina was shaking so badly the barrels were doing little circles like a double-headed snake ready to strike.

"You OK?" he said, fully out of breath.

She nodded. "You?"

"Hell, I don't know, do I look shot any place? They could have shot me and I didn't know it." He felt around on his person.

"Who are they, Bone?"

"Them god-damn' renegades!"

"They've come to kill us!"

Bone reached up and took the shotgun from her hands, afraid she might pull the triggers and blow his head off. "Jesus, woman!"

He eased himself to the window and looked out, didn't see a thing except rain, said: "I think maybe you run them off."

They waited in silence for a long time. Bone found himself a chair and sat in it, facing the front door, ready to kill anyone who came through it, the shotgun in his capable hands, fire racing through his blood like in the old days when he was young and skinny and full of piss. He found himself praying they'd come, hoping and willing for them to come

"Why'd you scream earlier?" he said, after an hour of sitting there waiting like that.

"I didn't know I did."

"I'll have to replace that back window you blowed out," he said. "Won't be hard to do if they got any glass at the hardware when I go in."

Rudina sat on the floor where Bone had told her to sit, her mind racing wildly and fretfully at the turn of events.

"Have to get some hinges, too, for the door," he said, trying to calculate the cost in his mind of new glass and hinges. "I wish now we'd quit this place a long time ago. Now I just got to put more money into it."

"Are you crazy?" she said.

"Hell, I must be. But crazy is all I got to go on right now. Crazy and this here god-damn' scatter-gun."

Rudina fell to a closed-eyed silence, and Bone willed men to come through his front door so he could kill them. The rain fell heavily for the next several hours, then he stopped wishing so hard when he heard a bird singing somewhere amid the trees. A bird or a wild renegade, he didn't know which, his mind was so full of crazy thoughts.

Sun pierced the busted window and lay in slabs across the floor. The shattered glass lay twinkling in the sunlight like precious stones. Bone felt stiff in his knees and hips from sitting so long, waiting for the men that never came. When he finally did try to stand up, he faltered and nearly fell back again.

The noise of his movement stirred Rudina and she opened her eyes and said: "I had a dream we were attacked by strange men and I shot out the windows and it all seemed so real." Then she looked around and saw that it wasn't a dream after all. "What time is it?" she said.

"I don't know, but it's sometime late afternoon, judging by the way the sun is angled," he said.

"Are you hungry, Bone?"

"You know, I think I could eat a preacher's mule."

He walked to the windows and looked out and saw nothing but sunlight on the rain-slick grass. The grass looked so brilliantly green that it hurt his eyes to look at it and that feeling welled up in his chest and brought tears to his eyes. He knew then how close they'd come to having been murdered. Had he left half an hour earlier, Rudina would have been alone. He knew from Jimmy all the terrible stories about what the renegades had done to women, especially women of police officers. He wondered if they had known he was a policeman and a friend of Jimmy Wild Bird's, or had they simply come upon the house by random, looking for some easy pickings? It caused him to go light in the head, that thought, and he leaned a hand against the doorjamb to steady himself. He didn't want to think about what would have happened and forced himself to concentrate only on what *did* happen. And the thing that happened was that he and Rudina had run off those sons-of-bitches, and he felt for once like a man instead of some fat old fool investigating the theft of stolen horses and breaking up marital spats.

He walked out into the yard to look for blood traces. Maybe he or Rudina had hit one of the renegades. He walked around and around the house, trying to see droplets of blood amid the raindrops clinging to the grass. He saw nothing. Then he looked up and saw a man astride a horse and was about to blow him out from under his hat when the man touched the brim of the frayed straw sombrero and said: "*Señor,* I'm looking for some men who might have come this way. Maybe you seen them, huh?"

CHAPTER THIRTY-FIVE

John Henry Cole rose early and dressed and went to the window and looked out. The sky was as blue and perfect as he'd ever seen it, but his mind was filled with thoughts about imperfect things in an imperfect world. Anna stirred amid the bedcovers, and he crossed the room and sat on the side of the bed.

She opened her eyes and looked at him and he could see she'd been crying. Cole remembered waking during the night to her stifled sobs.

"I have to go see now," he said.

"I want to go with you."

"OK, but only as far as Bone's. I'll see about renting us some horses to ride out there while you get dressed."

He started to stand. She took his hand. "I'm not blaming you," she said.

"Nobody's to blame," he said. "Bad things happen."

He left the room and descended the stairs and walked out into the brilliant morning. He was halfway down the street when he saw Bone Blue and Rudina. The buggy they rode in was rocking to and fro down the rutted street. Bone pulled up short when he saw Cole.

"Those renegades," he said. "I found 'em."

Something sharp caught under Cole's ribs. "You kill them?" he asked.

"No. But they damn' near killed me and Rudina."

"They found *you?"*

"Yeah. Whether they were looking for me or just looking to get lucky, I can't say."

"Anna's at the hotel," Cole said to Rudina. "Wonder if you'd mind going over there and being with her?"

She looked at Bone, and he nodded. She climbed down and crossed the street.

"There's something I have to tell you, Bone."

He wiped his upper lip with the back of his sleeve. "Something I got to tell you, too," he said.

Cole told him about Thomas being one of the renegades, about the possibility that he might have killed the boy back at Greasy Junction but couldn't be sure one way or the other.

Bone leaned off to one side and spat, wiped his upper lip again and said: "God damn, one of 'em's your and Anna's boy?"

Cole nodded, and Bone dismounted and tied up at a hitch rail, and said he needed a drink of something. They walked inside a restaurant that had freshly whitewashed walls and red-checkered tablecloths and the thick sweet smell of fatback frying.

A plump woman greeted them soon as they sat down, and Bone said: "Bring me some coffee, Minnie, and have Albert pour in some of that illegal whiskey he's been buying off those white peddlers."

"You know Albert don't break the law," she said.

Bone gave her a baleful stare until she turned and went into the kitchen. "What you going to do?" he asked Cole. "About them renegades and maybe your boy in among them?"

"I don't know exactly," Cole said. "But I can't kill my own son and I can't allow you to do it, either."

His eyes narrowed, the brown in them turning muddy. "Ain't so much me you have to worry about," he said. "An old Mexican calls himself Pablo Juárez is looking for them, too. He came by my place not long after the trouble, said he'd been tracking them for weeks. Said they killed his wife up in No Man's Land."

Cole remembered the name, the charred remains of the house, what Jimmy had said about the Mexican having once been a bandit. "Then we have to find him before this Juárez does," he said.

Bone sipped some of the coffee the waitress had brought and said: "That old man sounded serious as hell, and he must be a pretty damn' good tracker because he's followed them this far. I got the feeling there wasn't much going to stop him from killing them to the last one."

"All the more reason," Cole said.

"Let me ask you this," Bone said. "What if them boys don't give you no chance to take 'em alive? Then what?"

"I'll worry about that when the time comes. I got to get in the wind." Cole stood and started to leave.

Bone stood, too. "I'm going with you," he said. "It's gotten personal with me now, them trying to kill Rudina and me. . . ."

"I need to know you'll give him a chance to surrender, Bone."

"I can't promise if it comes down to my life or his. . . ."

"I'm not asking you to if it comes to that. Just give me a chance to take him alive."

Bone reached for his cup to drink down the last of his liquor-laced coffee, hitched his pants up over his belly, and said hurriedly: "We best not dawdle. That old Mexican sure as the hell probably ain't."

They rode out to Bone's and searched for tracks and saw only one fresh set, that of a single rider.

"I'm guessing it's the Mexican," Bone said.

"Then we follow."

"I don't see what the hell he's tracking, don't see no other tracks."

"If he's followed them from No Man's Land to here, he's onto them," Cole said.

They rode most of the day, heading north-by-northeast. Several times the trail skirted small towns, indicating the raiders were looking for something in particular, something easy, some farmer living out by himself. The bile rose in Cole's throat every time he thought about his own son being a rapist and a murderer. It wasn't the kind of thoughts a man should have to think about. They pressed on.

"We're in Creek country," Bone said late that afternoon. "Them boys is Creeks. Might have friends or relatives around."

"We find the Mexican first," Cole said.

"Sure, sure, we find the Mexican."

They did, near dusk, camped along a stream, squatting on his heels, watching their approach.

"*¡Hola!*" he said, and stood, a Winchester in his hands. "I know you been on my heels all day. Why you following me?"

Bone said: "You mind we squat and warm our hands?"

The Mexican nodded, and they stepped out of leather.

Cole took out the makings and offered them to the old man, but he waved off the offer. So he rolled himself a shuck and struck a match off his spur, cupping the flame against a wind that blew out of the northwest.

"What you want here?" the Mexican asked.

"We're looking for the same men you are," Cole said.

"I don't need no help, *señor*."

"We don't, either."

He looked up at the approaching night, the sky black silver, the North Star gleaming. "These men killed my wife," he said.

"One of them is my boy," Cole said.

His eyes narrowed. "That don't make no difference to me. They killed my wife."

"Maybe he didn't have a hand in it," Cole said.

"I was there. I saw my wife dead on the floor, saw what they had done to her. You think I don't know what they did?"

"You seen them do it? Every one of them had a hand in it?" Cole probed.

"I know what I saw," he said. "That's what I know."

"I want the chance to take him alive," Cole said.

"Then you better find him before I do."

Cole stared hard at him and saw no give in his eyes, no sign of mercy, and knew the Mexican was right. Cole had better find them before Pablo Juárez did.

CHAPTER THIRTY-SIX

The men ahead of him, the way they rode, heads down, tired, loose in the saddle, made Red Snake think of stray dogs, wild and mangy, looking for scraps to subsist on. He felt the last of his pride shimmer in his blood—like the wires of the telegraph shimmered in the fading sunlight. He wanted to ride away, drop off the trail, but there had been no opportunity to do it so far, and his was the poorest of the horses—assigned to him because he was the youngest among them. Caddo Pierce rode at the head of the group, Billy behind him, then Charley Fast Elk— each like a stray dog, looking, waiting to come on something or someone.

Red Snake felt the butt of his pistol pressing into his ribs, no shells in the chambers, none in the carbine of his saddle scabbard. That was why they hadn't kept up the attack on the last place—they'd run low on ammunition, naught but a handful of bullets between them. He was just as glad it had turned out that way. He had no heart to watch them kill another man, to ravish another woman. The creak of saddle leather, the ring of an iron shoe over loose rock, the jangle of bridle bit—sounds that reflected their poor, aimless state. Sounds of their demise, he thought.

Caddo was growing more cautious around the lot of them. Inwardly he knew that Billy would try and kill him as soon as they took care of the deputies, just as he planned to kill the kid. Billy boy had been grumbling, taking Charley off to the side and talking lingo to him. What he really couldn't figure was the boy. Red Snake was a spooky little bastard with a head full of strange thoughts. Hell, one way or the other, all these damned heathens were spooky. Yeah, he'd have to kill them all, but for now, their numbers reduced as they were, he wasn't foolish enough to reduce them further.

The boy saw a shooting star just as dusk turned to night and it reminded him of something that his mother had told him. She'd said that he was born on a night when the stars fell from the sky and he'd asked her how that was possible, and she'd said she didn't know, but that she'd seen it with her own eyes. He thought of her now as they rode along and wondered if she was up there somewhere among the stars. Maybe, if she was, she'd know he'd tried to keep his own hands from getting bloody.

He saw another star shoot across the sky, and it reminded him of the father he'd never known. His grandmother had told him that his father had fallen in a river trying to save a horse and had drowned the very morning of the day he was born. It seemed improbable to him such a thing might happen, and, when he was younger, he would go to the river she'd said his father had drowned in and sit along its banks, staring into the muddy water. And when he grew old enough and heard enough stories, he realized that his father had been a white man, because there was no denying that he had his father's gray eyes and none of the other Indian boys had gray eyes except him. And in this time of growing up, his mother had turned to drinking and telling men who came to see her their futures and some of the men would stay for a day or two, then ride off, and he would hear her weeping alone in her room, cursing their names. But all that didn't matter now. He'd begun preparing for his death, and if he were ever to meet his father, it would be in the hereafter, not in this life.

They topped a ridge and below lay the lights of a house, and they sat there for a moment until Caddo said: "Let's go taste some blood."

When Red Snake saw the flight of a crow across the moon, he knew this was the point where he would slip off into the night, and that's what he did, hanging back until they'd ridden out of sight and he saw from the ridge their shadows passing before the lights of the house, then he turned his pony's head back, and rode off to find his death.

CHAPTER THIRTY-SEVEN

Sometime during the night, the Mexican slipped away from the camp. John Henry Cole always slept light, a pistol in his hand under the blankets. Being both hunter and hunted had taught him caution. But he had not heard Pablo Juárez slip away.

Bone stirred awake, sat up, looked at Cole, looked around the camp.

"Get up!" Cole said to Bone.

By the time Bone had pulled on his boots, Cole was already saddling his horse. "He gone?" Bone asked, realizing why Cole was in a hurry

It took a few minutes to pick up Pablo Juárez's trail, but they found it on the other side of the small stream they'd camped near—the depressions of his horse's prints, cupped in the mud, a few bent cat-tails, that was it. He was on a line that took him north.

"That old man's like a ghost," Bone said.

Cole wasn't in any mood for palaver. He didn't know how much of a start the Mexican had on them, but even an hour was plenty.

They rode hard, lashing the withers of their mounts with the reins, but after an hour they still hadn't closed on him. They had to let up and allow their horses blow.

"Just because he jumped camp," Bone said, "don't mean he'll catch up to them afore we do."

"Wishful thinking," Cole said. "He'll catch them. He's got

245

their scent."

They allowed enough time for the mounts to rest, then stepped into leather again and continued on, but a mile later they lost his tracks crossing another tributary. Cole rode upstream, Bone down. They scouted the stream for ten minutes and didn't come on the old man's trail.

"He stayed in the water," Bone said. "What you want to do?"

"He'll come out somewhere and head north again. He's just making us kill more time."

They rode on.

It was late that afternoon when they topped a ridge and saw a house down below. There was a woman crossing from the barn to the house, her skirts billowing in the wind.

"What do you think?" Bone said.

"Hard to say."

"I don't see any horses. And I don't see that old Mexican's mount, either."

"Might have them in that barn yonder."

"Might."

The woman paused, looked toward the ridge where they sat their horses.

"You loaded for bear?" Cole asked.

"Damn' straight," Bone said, jerking the Winchester from his saddle boot.

"Let's go, then."

They rode down the slope. Cole saw the woman enter the house, then come back out again and stand on the porch, waving at them with one hand.

"Looks like she's friendly enough," Bone said.

It wasn't until they closed the distance to fifty yards that Cole saw the blood on her dress and the pistol in her hand. "Take cover!" he yelled, but a fusillade poured from the cabin window, and the air was shattered with busting glass and the whine of bullets as they tried to turn their horses.

First Bone's, then Cole's horse went down. They cleared leather just in time to keep from getting crushed by the falling horses.

"What the god-damn' hell!" Bone shouted as he scrambled to a position behind his dead mount, swiping sweat and dust from his eyes.

"It wasn't a woman!" Cole called to him. "It was one of the renegades in a dress!"

"Jesus!"

"Hold your fire!"

"What the hell for, so I can have plenty of bullets when those sons-a-bitches send me to the happy hunting ground?"

"You know what for!"

"I said only if it wasn't a matter of my life or his! It looks to me like that's what it's come to."

Cole sucked in a deep breath and looked over the pommel of his saddle, saw a smear of blood on the horn, realized he'd been nicked in the wrist by a bullet. He shucked his bandanna and wrapped the wrist. It felt numb.

From the house they laid down a withering fire for several minutes, the bullets thunking into the bodies of the dead horses. Bone snapped off shots in the direction of the house without really being able to raise himself enough to take aim.

"They skinned us," he declared.

"Not yet, they haven't."

A bullet took Bone's hat and sent it tumbling through the air. He cursed and fired two more shots up over his saddle without looking.

"You're just wasting your lead," Cole said.

"Tell *them* that."

"I'm telling *you* in case they keep us out here a long time."

Bone grunted.

247

"Might just as well wait for the sun to go down," Cole said, and laid his rifle aside, took out the makings, and rolled himself a shuck. Bone looked at the sky. It was lemon yellow. The sweat stained his face and he cuffed it out of his eyes.

"Come night, then what?" Bone queried.

"I ain't thought that far ahead yet."

He grunted again. "Well, at least we got to them before that Mexican bandit did."

Cole had it in his mind that they couldn't really have beaten Juárez to the house—he had had a good start on them and he wasn't that poor of a tracker. But if he wasn't down below, where exactly was he?

The firing from the house suddenly ceased. The two men lay there under the lemon-yellow sky, soaking in their sweat.

"It'll start to stink soon," Bone said. "These horses will bloat. Crows will come for their eyes. You ever smelled a dead horse?"

"Where you figure Juárez is?" Cole asked.

Bone peeked over his saddle at the house and a bullet ricocheted off his stirrup. "Don't reckon I give a shit," he replied, nearly breathless. "Unless he's on his way to save our bacon. You?"

"He should have beaten us here."

"Maybe he did."

"What do you mean?"

"Maybe he's inside, dead. Maybe he saw that renegade in the dress and thought it was some gal and they got him just like they almost got us. Maybe he just walked in on them and they killed him."

"I wouldn't count on it."

"I've got to make water," he declared.

"Better hold it until dark. They might shoot your whanger off."

Bone shifted his weight uncomfortably. "You got your canteen?"

"Best not to drink any more if you got to go," Cole cautioned.

"My throat's dry as sand and I lost my canteen on the way down."

Cole looked, saw that his own had two holes in it and the water had drained out.

"Look," Bone warned.

Cole gazed up at the lemon-yellow sky and saw a flight of crows.

"That ain't a good sign," Bone said.

"They're just crows."

"Crows is always a sure sign of bad things. Any Indian knows that."

Cole looked at the crows, the way their wings beat a steady flap against the lemon-yellow sky, saw the way the dying sun caught in their feathers, slick and black. Their shadows drifted over the ground below them, then they disappeared into a stand of trees beyond the house.

The sky went from lemon yellow to dusty rose.

"Be dark in less than half an hour," Cole observed.

"You figured out what then?"

"We'll try and catch them up."

"That's a damn' foolish thought."

"You got a better one?"

"Yeah, like hoofing back over that ridge and keep going till we get to that last town we saw."

"That's a good twenty miles," Cole reminded.

"I've walked farther."

"Darkness is the great equalizer."

"For who, us or them?"

"They won't think we'd come for them. They're probably thinking same as you, we'll hoof it out."

"It's craziness," Bone said. "And we *ought* to be hoofing it out."

"I'm through running, and you'd never make it twenty miles, all that weight hanging over your belt. A hundred yards to that house is a hell of a lot closer than that town. Besides, if we don't make a stand of it here, they'll ride us down and shoot us out in the open as easy as gophers. That the way you want to die? Like a gopher?"

"Don't want to die at all if I don't have to," he said, cuffing more sweat from his eyes.

They stretched out there for a time longer, and Cole went to roll another shuck before he realized he was out of tobacco. His mind was all over the thought of his boy being inside that cabin, and if he was . . . well, he didn't want to think about the outcome.

As if Bone were reading his mind, he said: "You might have to kill him."

Cole lay there, holding his rifle, thinking that Bone was right. He might have to kill his own son. In the end, he knew he couldn't do it.

The evening came on slowly, but when it arrived, it got dark in a hurry. A full moon rose over the stand of trees the crows had flown into and cast an eerie pale light over the land.

"Well?" Bone demanded. "What's your pleasure?"

"I'm going to sneak down there and see can I catch up their horses."

"We could sure use 'em."

"Can you hit anything with that long gun?" Cole asked.

"Shoot the balls off a cockroach."

Cole removed his spurs, left his rifle, and asked Bone for the belly gun he carried.

"Two-gun man, huh?" Bone said, seeing Cole pull his own revolver and check its loads.

"Try not to shoot anybody you don't have to," Cole said. "Me included."

Cole closed the distance to the barn, keeping low. There were no lights on inside the house, and the whole scene with the moon glow hanging over everything and the dazzling silence chilled his blood even though his shirt was soaked with perspiration. He slipped inside the barn, smelled horse and hay, heard the shuffle of their bodies as they shifted in their stalls. Beams of moonlight pierced the slats of the barn's walls and filtered down through the ill-repaired roof. There was enough light that he could make out five horses. He moved along their stalls, speaking to them in a low voice, unhitching the latches and turning them out. He found a couple of lead ropes and slipped them over the necks of two of the horses, climbed on the back of one, and herded the others toward the door, where they stood bunched up. He'd stolen horses in the past, away back when he was young and rowdy and living along the border. Stealing horses was a natural pastime for a poor cowpoke as long as you did it south of the Río Grande. Stealing north of the Río Grande could get you hanged.

Cole spoke to the ponies in Spanish, a lingo they seemed naturally to take to and one that soothes a horse right down. He rode in between the bunch, leading the one on a rope, pushed open the barn door, and rode out, the rest following like they'd been trained that way, and he walked them away from the barn and back toward Bone. When he got there, Bone looked at the string of horses and said: "Damn, you stole the whole bunch."

The horses didn't much care for the smell of death coming off the shot mounts and stamped about nervously until they led them off toward the stand of trees. Crows fluttered up from the limbs they'd been roosting in, then settled back again on new limbs, their black shapes silhouetted against the moon.

"Well, we got their horses," Bone said, "now what?"

"We wait."

"For them to come get 'em back?"

"Something like that."

They took shifts watching the house, two hours on, two off, until dawn.

When a gun-metal dawn did break across the horizon, Bone lay on his back snoring near the remuda of stolen horses. Cole had a good view of the house, maybe a hundred yards distant.

Soon a lone man came out, walked to the barn, entered, then went running back toward the house. Two others came out, pistols and rifles in their hands.

"Shoot the house," Cole said, kicking the soles of Bone's boots.

He sat up with a start. "Huh?"

"Shoot the house. I want them to know we're here and we're the ones got their horses."

They both took aim and fired into the walls of the house, and the men retreated inside.

"Damn, I think I may have wounded that house," Bone said sarcastically.

They waited, trapped in their own thoughts.

Time ticked off, then a man emerged from the house running toward the barn. Cole opened up, laying down a fire in front of him until he turned and retreated to the house again.

"Remind me not to enter you in no shooting matches," Bone said. "Unless it's a dirt shooting match."

"I want them to know they're trapped, and if they want out, they're going to have to surrender," Cole explained.

"Without water or food, we might have to surrender to them," Bone said.

"I thought Indians could go for weeks without food or water."

Bone looked at Cole. "Not us tame Indians," he said. "We got to eat. Especially us fat ones."

"You're a good man, Bone."

"Tell that to my widow when next you see her."

"You can tell her yourself when we get back."

Cole waited five minutes, then shouted toward the house: "United States deputy marshals out of Fort Smith! You men in the house surrender or we'll fire the house with you in it and shoot you coming out!"

Several more minutes went by, then a voice called out: "You god-damn' sons-a-bitches!"

Cole recognized the gravelly voice of Caddo Pierce. "Caddo! You and those boys give up, take your chances back to Fort Smith!"

"Not a god-damn' chance! Parker will hang us! Rather be shot than hanged!"

"Parker's not there any more, got a new judge, real easy fellow!" It was all lies, of course, but they didn't know it. "Better make up your mind, Caddo, these deputies are bloodthirsty, tired, and want to go home to their wives! They'll not wait past dusk!"

"You think they're buying that load of bull?" Bone asked quietly.

"Outlaws aren't the brightest bunch of yahoos ever to pull on their boots. Shoot the house some more."

They fired several more rounds into the walls of the house.

"Better pack it in, Caddo! I can't hold these boys back much longer!" Cole shouted.

"Deputies! Hell, all we counted was two of you yellow bastards!"

"Don't be a fool! I got twenty men caught up with me in the night! And every last one of them is a bloodthirsty son-of-a-bitch, just as soon see you and those boys dead as they would their own mammas! You better give it up quick, Caddo!"

"How we know you won't shoot us we come out?"

"You got my word!"

"Who the hell are you I should take your word?"

"Cole! John Henry Cole!"

There was a pause in the shouting conversation, then: "I thought Lucky Baker's wife killed you!"

"You coming out or do I let these boys get their way and fry your bacon?"

Another pause, then: "OK, OK, god damn it, don't shoot! We're coming out!"

"Hands held high!" Cole called. "Come out, then get down on your knees!"

Caddo stepped through the door first, followed by two slender Indian boys.

"I can't believe it," Bone said, when he saw them come out.

"Let's go catch them up," Cole said. "Stay alert until we got a rope on them."

They walked toward the house, and Caddo kneeled just as Cole had instructed him to do. Then one of the two Indian boys kneeled next to him. The third of them was hesitant and refused to kneel. Cole ordered him to get down. He looked across the span of space between them, then Cole saw him jerk the pistol from the back of his waistband and fire it into Caddo Pierce's skull.

"Shit!" Bone cried, followed by a roar that nearly took off Cole's ear as he fired his rifle.

The Indian boy buckled in the middle and toppled over next to Caddo Pierce who lay still, face down in the dirt.

Cole knocked the rifle from Bone's hands and ran forward, his pistol trained on the kneeling boy, who had a frightened stare in his brown eyes. The boy on the ground was writhing in pain. When Cole turned him over to look into his face, he saw that he, too, had brown eyes. Neither was his son.

"Where's the other boy?" he asked.

The dying Indian boy looked at Cole with all the hatred he could muster. "Go to hell, white man!" He gagged, spit blood, and moaned. Gut shot, he wouldn't last the hour.

Bone had come up, breathless, looked at Cole, and said: "Sorry as hell, but I couldn't take the chance he wouldn't pull down on us, too."

"He's not my boy," Cole said.

"Well, that's god-damn' good news, then. The other one?"

"No. Look at him."

Bone looked. "Pure Indian," he said. "Scrawny little Creek. What's your name, boy?"

"Charley Fast Elk, you big fat son-of-a-bitch!"

Bone backhanded him and said: "Show some god-damn' respect for the law."

Cole lifted the kid from the dirt and said again: "Where's the other boy who was with you?"

"Red Snake? Yellow bastard took off on us night before last. Billy was going to kill him anyway, so it didn't make no difference."

"Which way?"

He spat blood and dirt and looked at Cole sullenly. Then he looked at the dying boy near the white man.

"That the way you want your life to end, son?" Cole asked.

He pointed with his chin toward the ridge. "Up that way, I think."

Bone had gone inside the house, came out again, and said: "Jesus, there's a woman and a man dead inside. . . ."

Cole looked at the kid who called himself Charley Fast Elk and said: "Red Snake . . . he have anything to do with the rapes and murders?"

"What do you think?" he said sourly. "Chicken shit like him."

"Bone, you think you can take this one back to that little town and send someone back here to bury these people?"

255

"What you going to do?"

"Find the boy before the Mexican does."

"Get gone, then. I'll see you when you get back."

Cole rode hard for the ridge, and after a few minutes of scouting the area saw a set of single tracks leading off toward the west. Two miles later, he saw a second set of tracks following. The Mexican was on him.

CHAPTER THIRTY-EIGHT

Red Snake found a small stream that ran, clear and shallow, over smooth brown pebbles, and dismounted. He removed his clothes, the white man's clothes he wore—muslin shirt, denim trousers, scuffed boots, slouch hat. He placed these in a pile on the grassy bank and stood naked under the fading light, the sun setting beyond the low blue hills, its rays splayed out in sharp contrast.

He kneeled and swiped two fingers into the mud, just where the bank was cut away by the constant flow of water, and began streaking himself, face, shoulders, chest. From where he kneeled, he could see fish in a pool near a white rock, their speckled bodies wavering in the current as they waited for food to flow down to them. He moved to get a closer look and his shadow crossed the water, and they darted away.

He had begun to sing aloud now, the death song that had so long been kept inside him. He sang to the Great Father and to the Earth Mother. He sang to the forest creatures—the deer and wolf and fox—and begged their forgiveness for having killed so many of them. He sang to the Great Spirit that he felt descending upon him and took the knife from near the pile of clothing where he'd placed it and slashed his arms in mourning, cut off his hair, then took the hair and let the wind sweep it from his hands.

He sang and danced and called for the one who would kill him to come and give him a noble death. He saw blood raining from the sky. He felt the earth's heartbeat against the soles of his feet. He heard the cry of his brother, the coyote, and his sister, the hawk. He saw blackbirds gathered in the trees. He was through being a half white man. He was through being a half Indian. He would die an Indian who had rejected whatever white blood flowed through his veins. He kneeled by the stream and in that last brilliant light that is given off by the sun before it sinks beyond the horizon, he could see the gray eyes of his father—a man he'd never met, but one who he had always carried within his being. He sang curses to the man who'd given him life without giving him anything else.

Thump, thump. Thump, thump. Thump thump. A heartbeat turned into galloping hoofs. He turned about and saw the old man, sitting there atop a tall fine horse, his gaze narrowed—an old wolf watching a prairie chicken.

The last bit of sun glinted off the brass bands of the old man's rifle that rested across the pommel of his saddle. "What you doing, eh?" the old man said.

Red Snake did not answer for he knew there was no answer that the old man would understand. "You've come to kill me," he said.

The old man nodded, once.

"Then do it!"

The old man spurred his horse closer as though to get a better look at him.

"The gray eyes . . . ," the man said almost thoughtfully. "I remember you now."

Red Snake stood with his arms outstretched, his death song rising from his chest, guttering in the back of his throat, sliding forth in a mournful wail.

"You were the one who came back and cut me free . . . I remember now. . . ."

Red Snake paused in his singing, then he, too, remembered

the old man, the one whose woman they'd killed up in the distant place they called No Man's Land, the one he had released to go and care for his dead wife in a proper way. Why he'd done it, even Red Snake wasn't sure. "No," he said. "You are mistaken, mister."

The old man's horse shifted its rear hoofs and stepped sideways. "You were one of them," he man said. "One who killed my wife. . . ."

"Yes. I was one of them," Red Snake said. "You must take my life now for what I've done."

He saw the old man raise his rifle, saw the blooded eye sighted down the barrel at him, and prepared himself for the bullet. The old man steadied the horse with his knees.

"Go ahead," Red Snake said. "It will be an honorable death."

There in the twilight they stood, the boy, his arms outstretched in a way that reminded Pablo Juárez of the stone Christ he'd seen in the church of his boyhood village. A drop of sweat fell into Pablo's eye and blurred his vision, and he wiped it clear. The boy stood, his head thrown back, his arms slashed and bleeding, mud streaks over his face and chest. Pablo felt a faint pain rise up under his breastbone and squeeze his breath. A crow cawed from a tree limb, its body dark against the black-silver sky. The rifle grew heavy in Pablo's hands, and he lowered it and let it rest there on the pommel of his saddle again. The boy lowered his head and stared at him.

"Go ahead, old man, why do you hesitate?"

"I need to get off my horse first," Pablo said.

"Then do it," the boy said, thinking that the old man meant he needed to stand in order to shoot him.

Pablo Juárez felt as though his soul had suddenly fled him, taking with it the last bit of strength in his bones. The flame of pain in his chest grew more intense as he slid from the saddle and steadied himself against the ribs of his horse. "Tell me this one thing," Pablo said. "Why did you kill my wife? What did you need to do that for?"

The boy felt the flush of humiliation. "She was killed for no reason," he said.

Pablo closed his eyes for a moment, trying to absorb the hot pain in his chest and the ringing of the boy's words in his ears. "I don't believe you had a hand in it," he said. "I think, if you helped kill my wife, you would have not come back and set me free."

"Don't be foolish," the boy said. "I was as much a part of it as any of them."

"No," Pablo said. "I think you got mixed up with some bad *hombres* and you rode with them as far as you could, and when you couldn't go any farther with these men, you left and went on your own because you were too ashamed of what they had done."

"I've come here to die," the boy said.

"Not by my hand."

"Yes, you are the one I have sinned against, you must be the one to bring about my death."

Pablo felt the pain clutching his heart so that he could hardly take a breath. The face of his wife swam before his eyes. "Why do you want to die?" he asked the boy.

"Because I have nothing to live for."

"Then find someone else to kill you. . . ." Pablo saw a stump and went and sat upon it, feeling the weakness in his legs now, the slight numbing of his left arm and hand. The boy saw how the old man looked under the dying light, his face as ashen as winter sky. He knew the look meant death would come soon for the old man. But he must not let it come too soon. He strode to his pile of clothes and found the pistol. Knowing that there were no bullets in it, he brought it around and aimed it Pablo. Old instincts took over, old reflexes that seemed to come from the ancient history of Pablo's being, and just as he raised the rifle and pulled the trigger, he heard someone call: "No. Don't!"

CHAPTER THIRTY-NINE

John Henry Cole came through the trees just as the old man was raising his rifle. He saw a pistol in Thomas's hand, aimed at the old man, who was sitting on a stump. Night was closing in fast and the distant sky showed the color of blood-tinged water. Cole yelled for the old man to hold off, but his scream was matched only by the crack of Pablo's rifle. The boy spun and dropped like a stone. In that moment of insanity, Cole's own world went nearly black.

He leaped from his horse and kneeled by the boy and raised his head. His gray eyes fluttered open and looked into Cole's. The front of his shirt billowed into a crimson flower. He stared into Cole's eyes for a long full moment, then said: "You came too late. . . ."

Cole saw that the shot had missed the boy's heart by inches. Inspecting further, he saw the bullet had passed through him cleanly. If he could stop the flow of blood, he might yet save him. He pulled the bandanna from around his neck and plugged the bloody hole. Thomas's breathing became labored. The bullet could have struck the top of his lung, and, if it had, he would die before Cole could get help.

Cole looked toward the old Mexican who was sitting on the stump, only now his rifle had fallen from his hands and his body had slumped into a question mark. "I did not want to shoot him . . . ," Pablo Juárez said, his voice trembling. "But when I saw him aim his pistol. . . ."

"I know," Cole said.

"He didn't ever do nothing to me. . . ." Then Pablo Juárez fell from the stump and did not move.

Cole had no way to bury him, so later he would gather rocks from along the stream and build a stone cairn over him that would keep the crows away. First he had to attend to his son. He built a fire and took out his knife and held the blade in the flames until it glowed redly. Thomas watched him with wildly expectant eyes.

"This is going to hurt like hell," Cole said, taking the blade from the fire. "But it's the only way I can stanch the blood and keep you from bleeding to death."

CHAPTER FORTY

Anna Wild Bird was on the porch when they arrived. She saw Thomas sitting next to Cole on the wagon seat. Cole thought that she knew, even at a distance, that it was their son. For a long time she just stood there, and the boy said: "Is that her?"

"Your mother," Cole said.

"I don't know what to say to her," he said.

"You don't have to say anything."

In the days since Cole had found the boy, he had taken him to a doctor, then on the return journey to Talaquah. Thomas had been a brooding, confused kid who asked few questions. Cole thought he already knew most of the answers, but he had told him who he was, and he had told him that he had only learned about him recently, and that he was sorry for everything that had happened to him.

"You're still a lawman," the boy had said at one point.

"*Was* a lawman," Cole had corrected.

"You're still a white man. . . ."

"That I can't change. Neither can you. We have to deal with the hand that's been dealt to us . . . you, me, your mother. . . ."

"You going to be the one to take me to Fort Smith for my hanging?"

"You do something you deserve to be hanged for?"

"I rode with those men while they murdered people, raped women. . . ."

"Did you have a direct hand in it?"

He hadn't looked at Cole.

"Whether you did or not," Cole had said, "I won't take you to Fort Smith. Maybe somebody else will want to, but it won't be me."

Then the boy had looked at Cole, looked into his eyes, and Cole had seen a boy who was afraid and confused and ashamed.

"I never killed any of them. It made me sick, what they did."

They pulled up in the yard. Anna's hand went to her mouth when she got a closer look at him. "Thomas . . . ?"

He looked at the toes of his boots.

Cole climbed down and went to her. "Give him some time."

Tears welled in her eyes.

"He's got a gunshot wound. He'll need time to recover," Cole said.

Her gaze went from Thomas to Cole.

"He knows everything," Cole said.

She crossed the yard and stood next to the wagon. "Do you want to get down, rest on the porch? Are you hungry?"

Thomas shook his head.

She touched his leg as gently as if she expected him to shy away like a wild thing. "There's so much we need to talk about . . . ," she said.

"Why don't you go on in the house and rest some," Cole said to Thomas.

He slid from the wagon seat, still favoring the wound, and went slowly into the house.

"Did he . . . ?" she began.

"No, he didn't have anything to do with the killings," Cole assured. He took her in his arms, noting the stiffness of her body. "I brought him back to you, Anna. It's the only thing I could do."

She looked toward the house. "It will take us time to get to know each other," she said.

Cole nodded. "It's a lot to chew for all of us." He kissed her forehead and stepped up onto the wagon.

"Where are you going?" she asked.

"I've got something to do. And, besides, I think you and Thomas need to be alone together for a time."

"Are you coming back?"

"Is that what you want?"

The uncertainty floated into her gaze. "I'm still a widow," she said. "I'll need time to grieve for Jimmy, and Thomas will need me. . . ."

"Let's both give it some time," Cole said. "Then I'll get back up this way and see how things are between us."

"Thank you," she said, her voice as soft as a morning sky.

Cole looked into her eyes one more time, took up the reins, and turned the horses' heads toward town.

In Talaquah, Bone Blue was in his office when Cole arrived. Cole told him the story.

"Might be some want to hold him accountable," Bone said.

"He didn't have a rôle in it. Let it go. Nobody has to know but us."

"Hell, I'm quitting the law anyway," Bone said. "Rudina wants me to become a farmer, raise beans and squash. What about you?"

Cole asked him if he would look after Anna and Thomas, maybe be an uncle to the boy while Cole was gone.

"You ever going to lose them wings off your feet?" Bone said.

"Someday soon, I hope," Cole said.

"Where you going to now?"

"See a man about some angels," Cole said.

★ ★ ★ ★ ★

The headstone Cole placed over the grave read:

PABLO JUÁREZ
A MAN WHO LOST EVERYTHING
BUT HIS HONOR

He stood back and admired the pair of winged angels he'd had the stone mason carve just above the name. They looked like their wings were strong enough to carry a man to the happy hunting grounds, maybe to that place where they'd carried his wife.

Then Cole hoisted a bottle of tequila and drank one for the old bandit before setting it down against the headstone.

"You take care, *hombre,* and have one or two on me on your journey."

ABOUT THE AUTHOR

Bill Brooks is the author of twenty-five novels of historical and frontier fiction. After a lifetime of working a variety of jobs, from shoe salesman to shipyard worker, Brooks entered the health care profession where he was in management for sixteen years before turning to his first love—writing. Once he decided to turn his attention to becoming a published writer, Brooks worked several more odd jobs to sustain himself, including wildlife tour guide in Sedona, Arizona where he lived and became even more enamored with the West of his childhood heroes, Roy Rogers and Gene Autry. Brooks wrote a string of frontier fiction novels, beginning with *The Badmen* (1992) and *Buscadero* (1993), before he attempted something more lyrical and literary in the critically acclaimed: *The Stone Garden: The Epic Life of Billy the Kid* (2002). This was followed in succession by *Pretty Boy: The Epic Life of Pretty Boy Floyd* (2003) and *Bonnie & Clyde: A Love Story* (2005). *The Stone Garden* was named by *Booklist* as one of the top ten Westerns of the decade. After that trio of novels, Brooks was asked to return to frontier fiction by an editor who had moved to a new publisher and he wrote in succession three series for them, beginning with *Law For Hire* (2003), then *Dakota Lawman* (2005), and finishing up with *The Journey of Jim Glass* (2007). *The Messenger* (Five Star, 2009) was Brooks's twenty-second novel. *Blood Storm* (Five Star, 2011) was the first novel in a series of John Henry Cole adventures. It was praised by *Publishers Weekly* as a well-crafted story with an added depth due to its characters. Brooks now lives in northeast Indiana. His next Five Star Western will be another John Henry Cole story titled *Men of Violence*.